WILD REK

Wilder Series 4

Sandy Sullivan

EROTIC ROMANCE

Siren Publishing, Inc.
www.SirenPublishing.com

Lyn,
this is
the last
one. Enjoy!
Sandy
Sullivan

A SIREN PUBLISHING BOOK
IMPRINT: Erotic Romance

WILD REKINDLED LOVE
Copyright © 2010 by Sandy Sullivan

ISBN-10: 1-60601-747-0
ISBN-13: 978-1-60601-747-0

First Printing: August 2010

Cover design by Jinger Heaston
All cover art and logo copyright © 2010 by Siren Publishing, Inc.

Printed in the U.S.A.

PUBLISHER
Siren Publishing, Inc.
www.SirenPublishing.com

DEDICATION

This book is dedicated for the fans of the Wilder Series. This is the final chapter and I hope you all have enjoyed reading this series as much as I enjoyed writing it.

AUTHOR'S NOTE

I hope you have all enjoyed reading about the Wilder family and their bumpy road to love throughout the Wilder Series.

This family took root in my imagination with nothing more than the first scene where Abby is sitting at the window crying.

I've laughed and cried with them through all four of their stories and I hope you did the same. There were several instances while I wrote a couple of special scenes, that I had to stop. I couldn't see through my own tears, but I'm glad they all have their happily ever after.

WILD REKINDLED LOVE

Wilder Series 4

SANDY SULLIVAN
Copyright © 2010

Chapter One

"Okay, folks. This is our own little hometown girl, Samantha Wilder. She is one of the best little barrel racers I've seen in a long time. Let's give it up for her and cheer her on. Go get 'em, Sam!"

"You heard him, baby. Go get 'em." Jamie smiled from next to Samantha's horse.

"Aw, Mom," Samantha grumbled before she kicked her mare and moved away.

Jamie took her place at the fence as Sam started her run. She made the first turn with a great time, but when she headed for the second barrel, she lost her balance and tumbled to the ground. Jamie hopped the fence and took off at a dead run toward her daughter. When she reached her side, Samantha lay in the dirt crying and holding her left arm.

"Oh, God. Sammy, are you all right?"

"Mommy, my arm hurts."

"It's okay, baby. Hold on. The paramedics will be here in a jif."

Jamie wiped the tears cutting a path down her daughter's dirty cheeks. She knew if Sam cried, she must really be hurt and she didn't like the angle of her arm.

A moment later, Jamie's brother, Chase, stood at her side.

"Hey, squirt. What did you do now?"

"Uncle Chase, my arm hurts."

"Let me look, sweetie."

"What do you think? Is it broken?"

"I'm not a doctor, sis, but I would say yeah. The paramedics will take her to the hospital and get it x-rayed. That way we'll know for sure."

"Hey, Chase. What do we have?"

"Looks broken, but you guys are the experts."

"That would be my guess too with the angle. We'll take her in, Jamie. She'll be fine. You can ride up front."

"Thanks, Jack." Jamie turned to her brother while the paramedics splinted Samantha's arm and put her on the stretcher. "Can you get my truck to the hospital for me?"

"No problem, sis. I'll drive it and Abby can pick me up."

I'll see you there, then," Jamie said before she turned to follow behind her daughter.

* * * *

"Doctor Crossland?"

Wyatt Crossland looked up from the chart he had under his hand to find Amy Jenkins, registered nurse, standing at the entrance of the dictation room. "Yes?" She smiled.

She is kind of pretty with her big blue eyes, but she's not the one I want.

"We have an ambulance coming in from the rodeo and a couple more patients in triage. The physician's assistant is asking for you."

"All right. I'll be right there." He rubbed his tired eyes for a moment before he struggled to his feet. It had been a hellacious twenty-four hours. The day before, the emergency room had been so busy, he hadn't gotten any rest at all and when he went home, he had slept like the dead, not even waking for the alarm. The hospital had to call him and wake him up for his shift.

He made his way to the nurse's station and stopped to talk to the physician's assistant before he grabbed a chart. Flipping through the triage sheet, he sighed before he turned and headed toward the patient waiting.

Walking into the small room where his next patient lay, he vaguely heard the ambulance roll in and one of the nurses direct the paramedics to a trauma bay.

Mrs. Lewis lay stretched out on the gurney in front of him, telling him about the pain in her hip that had been there for over a month.

I love emergency medicine, but Lord sometimes I wish I didn't have to listen to the same complaints day in and day out.

"Well, Mrs. Lewis, we'll x-ray it and make sure nothing is broken, but it sounds more like arthritis pain. I'll put in the order for the x-ray and something for pain for you. Okay?"

"Of course, Wyatt. You were always such a nice boy when you were growing up." The elderly lady patted his cheek affectionately. "Too bad you had to leave to go off to school, but you are home now."

"Thanks ma'am. I'll be back to see you in a bit."

"You just take your time, son. I know you're busy."

"Yes ma'am."

He stepped out of the room and sighed.

This was a mistake. Why the hell did I ever come back to Laramie in the first place? His heart whispered in return, *because she's here.*

Amy handed him a chart and said, "You might want to see this one next. It's a little nine-year-old girl who fell at the rodeo and I'm pretty sure her radius is broken. I've ordered x-rays already, but she's hurting pretty bad and her mother is upset too."

"Okay. Thanks, Amy."

The nurse's eyes held a promise—the promise of fun later if he so chose. "No problem. Call me if you need anything."

Nine years old. That's just about the age our daughter would be. Stop, Wyatt! Just stop! He shook his head before he headed in the direction of trauma bay five. Approaching the curtained off area, the soft murmurs of voices reached his ears and his heart skipped a beat. He looked at the chart in his hands, noting the name at the top. Samantha Wilder. *Holy fuck! It can't be!*

He took an unsteady step back as his gaze shot to the curtain again. *Shit! I can't go in there, I just can't.*

"You okay, doc?" the male technician asked when he stopped at Wyatt's side.

His stare swung to the other man and he mumbled, "Yeah. I'm fine."

Taking a huge deep breath to steady his nerves, he slipped inside the curtained off area to meet the startled brown eyes of the woman he had left behind over nine years before.

God, she looks good.

Womanly curves graced her hips now that hadn't been there before, but she still sported shoulder length wavy hair, full kissable lips, straight nose and breasts he would love to taste again.

"Hi, Jamie."

Her startled gasp whipped through the air around them before she jumped to her feet. "Wyatt?" She took a step toward him. "Oh, my God! Wyatt!"

Jamie threw her arms around his neck and his hands immediately went to her waist. He closed his eyes for a moment as he inhaled the sweet scent of roses and horse. He would forever link the two with Jamie.

After several seconds, embarrassment flushed her cheeks before she dropped her arms and stepped back. "I'm sorry."

"Nothing to be sorry for."

"What are you doing here? I mean—wait! You're the doctor in the emergency room? Since when?"

"Can we talk about this later? I need to treat your daughter."

Jamie turned and moved back toward the other side of the bed. "She fell at the rodeo. I think her arm is broken."

Wyatt's eyes moved over the beautiful little girl on the gurney and his heart swelled in his chest. *My daughter.* "Hi, sweetie. I'm Doctor Crossland, but you can call me Wyatt." *Or Dad.* "Can I look at your arm?"

Samantha's lips turned down in a frown as she held her arm to her chest. "It hurts."

"I know it does, pumpkin, but I need to see it so we can make it feel better."

His heart thumped loudly at the trust in the blue eyes so much like his own. If he had any doubt the little girl in front of him happened to be his daughter, it vanished when he noted the color of her eyes. The turquoise blue was a trademark of the Crossland family.

"Okay," Samantha said.

He gently grasped her arm and then ran his fingers along the area appearing to be fractured and she whimpered slightly as she tried to pull her arm out of his grasp. "It's okay. I'm almost done."

"Mom?"

"It will be fine, Sammy. He won't hurt you," Jamie said, their eyes meeting over their daughter's head, before he returned to the task at hand.

"There you go, sweetie." He gently laid her arm back across her chest. "A nice young lady is going to take some pictures for me, okay?"

He could see tears welling up in her eyes, but she refused to let them fall when she stubbornly nodded. *Just like her mother.*

"Jennifer, just get a two view of the forearm, especially right there," he pointed to the large lump under the skin.

"No problem, doc." The young x-ray technician turned to Samantha and said, "Can you walk with me, sweetheart, or do you want to take a ride in a chair?"

"How about the chair, Jen? I'm sure Samantha will enjoy it."

"Okay. Got one right here." Jennifer pulled the wheelchair up closer to the bed and said to Jamie, "You can come too, mom."

The trio moved down the hall toward x-ray while Wyatt stood outside the trauma bay curtain and watched. A confused looked crossed Jamie's face before they rounded the corner and disappeared.

* * * *

What in the hell is he doing here? Nine years! It's been nine years since he held me in his arms and now he's back and just as devastating to my heart as before. Damn, he looks fantastic. The full head of dark hair was slightly longer than she remembered and when she'd thrown herself against his chest, the familiar rock hard muscles felt good, too good. Standing six-foot, he always made her feel almost petite even at her own five feet eight inches tall. Polo cologne wrapped itself around her mind when he'd held her for that split second, taking her back to a time when things were so much simpler. Jamie closed her eyes and sighed before she rubbed a spot over her left eye where a nagging headache had begun to pound.

Shit! Chase will kill him, not to mention Cole and Justin if they get wind he's back in town.

The radiology technician handed her a heavy apron to put over her chest so she could stay in the room with Samantha.

Damn! Samantha! How am I going to explain this to her? Of course, Wyatt didn't say anything. I wonder if he thinks she's not his—no, he can't possibly think that. She's got his eyes.

"If you'll stand over there against the wall, Mom, I'll get these pictures really fast and we'll be done."

"Sure. Thanks for being so good to her."

"No problem. She's a doll."

Once they were finished, Jennifer rolled them back to the room they were in before and Samantha hopped up on the bed again, cradling her arm to her chest. "Where is Wyatt, Mom?"

Wyatt.

"I'm sure he'll be back in here in a minute, sweetie. He has to look at the pictures to make sure what is wrong with your arm."

In her best grown up voice, Samantha said, "Mom? Did you know him before?"

Jamie's heart stopped in her chest, and she looked her daughter. "What makes you say that, Sam?"

"You hugged him."

More like threw myself into his arms.

"Yeah, sweetie, I knew him a long time ago. He's been gone for awhile."

"Did he know my Dad?"

Jamie closed her eyes for a moment before she looked at her daughter again.

What the hell do I say to that?

"Yeah, Sammy, he knew your Dad."

A moment later, Wyatt stepped through the curtain and she knew by the confusion on his face he had heard the conversation between her and Samantha.

"Well, it is broken and we'll have to put a splint on her arm."

"You'll give her something for pain?"

His mouth turned down in a frown. "Of course, Jamie. I would never do anything to hurt her."

No, but you walked out on her before she was ever born!

"Good."

His focus turned back to their daughter. "Sweetheart? We are going to have to see if we can fix that arm." Samantha nodded. "I'm going to give you a shot with some medicine so it won't hurt."

Samantha's eyes widened and she looked at Jamie. "A shot?"

"It's okay, Sammy. I'm right here, sweetie. It will only hurt for a little bit. Like if Jeremiah pinched you."

"Jeremiah?" Wyatt asked.

"Chase and Abby's son—her cousin."

Confusion rippled across his face.

"A lot has changed since you've been gone."

"Obviously."

"You know my Uncle Chase?" Samantha asked when her gaze pinned Wyatt where he stood.

Wyatt nodded and said, "I used to, anyway. I haven't seen any of them in a long time."

"That's probably a good thing."

He frowned again and cocked his head to the side.

The nurse came in behind him and moved toward Samantha with the injection in her hand. Samantha whimpered, making Jamie's heart clench.

"It'll be okay, sweetie. Do you want me to hold your hand?" he whispered when he sat down on the chair next to her bed and scooted closer. Samantha nodded and Jamie frowned. "Be gentle," he said with a pointed stare at the nurse. "Roll on your side, pumpkin, toward me." Samantha did as he asked and he grasped her small hand in his. "Jamie, hold her legs so she doesn't kick."

Her mouth turned down at the corners, but did as he asked, positioning herself across Samantha's legs. As the nurse stuck the injection in and slowly pushed the medication, Jamie could see the tears well up in Samantha's eyes, but the little girl's gaze never left Wyatt's face.

"Almost done," he whispered.

Jamie felt her heart crack.

Damn it! He shouldn't be connecting with her like this, not after deserting us.

The trust in Samantha's eyes when she stared into Wyatt's until the nurse finished, hurt Jamie to watch. "See. It wasn't that bad, huh."

Samantha shook her head 'no' as she rolled back on her back.

His gaze returned to Jamie's and he stood. "We'll give it a few minutes for the medication to kick in and relax her before I set her arm."

Jamie nodded, but didn't speak. Anger, betrayal, distrust and what, she didn't know, rippled through her as she moved back up to Samantha's side.

His lips pulled tight across his mouth when their eyes met and frown lines settled between his eyebrows. "I'll be back in a little bit, pumpkin."

"Okay, Wyatt."

Her eyes met his for a moment before he turned and left the room without another word.

"You okay?"

Samantha nodded. "My arm hurts, though."

"I know, sweetie, but they just gave you some medicine that should help."

"Am I going to get a cast?"

"Yep. Afraid so."

Samantha smiled and the tell-tale Wilder dimples flashed in her cheeks as her turquoise eyes danced. The medication began to take effect and Jamie could see Samantha's features relax. "It will be kind of cool though, Mom. None of my friends have had a cast before."

Jamie smiled as her eyes caressed the beautiful face of her daughter and she brushed the hair off her forehead. "Leave it to you to think this is something to be proud of."

"Mom?"

"Yeah, baby."

"I like Wyatt. He's cool." Jamie's heart tripped over in her chest when Samantha's words met her ears. "I wonder if my Dad was that cool."

Tears burned the back of Jamie's eyes a moment before she closed them a minute and kissed her daughter's forehead. "He was, baby," she whispered.

Wyatt returned a few minutes later and Samantha had drifted off to sleep. "You can wait outside if you want."

"No, I'll stay with *my* daughter."

His gaze met hers a moment before his shoulder lifted in a half-shrug. "Suit yourself." Moving to the little girl's side, he lifted her arm and she pulled against his grasp even in her sleep. He bent down and whispered something in her ear that Jamie couldn't hear before he stood up again. His hands moved to the bump under the skin of her forearm and he ran his thumbs over it before pushing softly.

Samantha whimpered when he gently manipulated the bones back into place.

"There. That should do it. The nurse will put a temporary splint on until you can take her to an orthopedic doctor for a regular cast."

He moved toward the curtain but stopped when she said, "Wyatt?"

"Yeah?"

She dropped her eyes a moment and bit her lip before they returned to his. "Thanks."

"You're welcome." With a look in his eyes she couldn't read, he smiled and then disappeared out through the curtains.

Chapter Two

She didn't see Wyatt again except for a brief glimpse before they left the rear of the emergency room. Their eyes met across the desk for a split second and her heart dropped into her stomach. She could finally breathe again once they reached the large waiting room.

Her worried gaze met that of her brother and Abby.

"Everything okay?"

"Yeah. Sam will be fine. She's tired now because they gave her something for pain so they could set the arm." Jamie pushed the wheelchair out toward her truck with Chase and Abby on her heels. Avoiding a confrontation between Chase and Wyatt, was utmost in her mind.

"It is broken, then?"

"Yeah."

"Poor kid," Chase said as he brushed the hair off Samantha's forehead. "Let's get her home, so she can sleep."

"That would be a great idea," Jamie said and Chase frowned.

"Is there something wrong?"

A quick glance over her shoulder at the doors of the emergency room revealed nothing. "No. Why would you say that?"

"You seem kind of wound up, that's all."

"I'm just still worried about Samantha, Chase."

"Did the doctor give you something to worry about?"

Other than the fact that you will kill Wyatt when you find out he's in town? Or that he bonded with his daughter without her even knowing who he is? "No. He said she would be okay and I want to get her home."

Jamie opened the truck and Chase lifted his niece into his arms before sliding her into the cab and buckling her seatbelt. "We'll see you back at moms, then. Abby and I were headed there tonight for dinner anyway."

"Sure. See you there." Once she made it inside the truck, she let out the breath she'd been holding and finally relaxed a moment.

God, please don't let my brothers find out Wyatt is back before he and I have a chance to talk. I need to find out why he's here. The way Chase, Justin and Cole searched for him after he disappeared he had to know he wouldn't be welcome. Confusion rippled across her mind. Air rushed from between her lips in a heavy sigh and she shook her head to clear her thoughts. *This is the last thing I need right now.*

The truck started with a turn of the key and she backed out of the stall before she pulled out onto the highway headed for home. Her gaze found her sleeping daughter in the seat next to her and she smiled. Samantha favored her father so much in her looks, it hurt Jamie's heart to see it sometimes. The brown semi-wavy hair and dimples came from her mother, but the shape of her face and her penetrating eye color came from her father.

Wyatt. What the hell am I going to do about him? I have a gut feeling he is going to want to be a part of her life now. Frown lines appeared between her eyes. *Just because he's back in town doesn't give him the right to decide he all of the sudden wants to be a father to her!*

Jamie pulled the truck into her parent's driveway and Chase parked behind her before he moved toward the passenger side of her truck. "I'll carry her in."

"I'll get the door." The door opened with the pressure of her hand and she stopped to hold the screen as he moved inside with Samantha cradled in his arms. "Take her on up to her room. She'll probably sleep until dinner." When her brother disappeared, she looked at Abby and frowned. The twinkle in her sister-in-law's eyes made Jamie pause. "What?"

With a secretive smile gracing her lips, Abby cocked an eyebrow in her direction and said, "Nothing."

"Nosy sisters," Jamie grumbled before she disappeared into the kitchen for something to drink, but she thought for sure she heard Abby chuckle behind her. Abby's gift was well known and unfortunately, it seemed she now happened to be the target of that gift. Chase had Abby, Cole had Carrie and Justin was setting up house and home with Katrina. Now being the only unattached Wilder left, she knew Abby had her sights set on seeing Jamie happily settled down with a spouse or significant other of her own. She didn't think Abby knew about Wyatt except what Chase had told her, but she wouldn't be at all surprised if her sister-in-law knew all about him.

I just hope she hasn't sensed the meeting at the hospital. I might have to talk to her when Chase isn't around.

With the beer she'd retrieved from the refrigerator in her hand, she headed back into the living room just in time to see Chase return from putting Samantha in her room. "She still asleep?"

"Yep. Snug as a bug."

"Good."

"Jamie?" Bonnie called from the den.

"Yeah, Mom?"

"You better call Ashley. She's called several times since the accident."

"All right." Jamie grabbed the phone and dialed Samantha's friend. She made sure the other little girl knew Sam would be fine, but she had a broken arm and wouldn't be playing for at least a couple of days. "You can come over and see her tomorrow, okay? She's resting now." After another minute or so, she hung up the phone, grabbed her beer and sat down next to Abby while Jeremiah ran around their legs.

"So they said she would be okay?" Chase asked.

A sigh rushed from between her lips and she leaned her head back on the couch cushion. "She'll be fine, Chase. I have to take her to an orthopedic doctor in the next couple of days to put a permanent cast on, but for now, she's fine. Quit worrying." Leveling him with an exasperated look, she said, "Damn! You act like her father."

"Well, someone has to, since Wyatt skipped town."

"I can take care of *my* daughter just fine, thank you."

"Yeah, that's why you're living with Mom and Dad."

She stood up angrily and shouted, "Fuck you, Chase! I may not have a place of my own yet, but I still can take care of Samantha when I need to."

He rose to his feet too and stopped in front of her, grasping her shoulders in his hands. "I'm not saying you can't. All I'm saying is that she should have a father figure and I feel like that responsibility lies with me since her real dad didn't have the balls to stick around."

"Mom?" The adults turned only to find Samantha standing on the stairs, rubbing her eyes.

"I'm sorry, baby. Did we wake you?"

"No, not really. My arm is starting to hurt again."

"Let me get you some of the medicine the doctor said you could have, okay?"

Samantha nodded and Jamie disappeared into the kitchen to retrieve the medication Wyatt has prescribed for her pain. When she returned, she found her daughter sitting on the couch next to her uncle and her heart stopped when she heard Samantha's words.

"The doctor at the hospital said he knew you, Uncle Chase, or did a long time ago. And Mom knew him, too. She even hugged him when he first came into my room."

"Really? What was his name, Sammy?"

"Wyatt."

Chase's gaze ricocheted up to hers and she felt the color drain out of her cheeks as her hands began to shake.

"Wyatt?" His blue eyes narrowed into agitated slits and her knees went weak.

"Yep. He's cool. He took really good care of me and even sat down and held my hand while they gave me medicine."

"Care to explain, sis?"

"Um…no."

"Jamie Marie?" he growled.

"Don't give me that shit, Chase. I'm *not* discussing this in front of Samantha."

"Fine." He stood and grabbed her arm around her bicep as he physically escorted her through the kitchen and out the back. "Wyatt?"

"Don't start, brother."

"He's here?" He raked his fingers through his hair before he started to pace. "That son of a bitch is here! In Laramie?"

"Yes, he is."

"He's a doctor? At the fucking emergency room?"

"Evidently."

He stopped in front of her and grabbed her arm in another fierce grip. "Did you know he was here?"

"Of course I didn't, not until he walked into her room." Her voice rose in agitation.

Damn him!

"I'll kill him!" Chase growled as he headed for the house.

He stopped when Jamie said, "Leave him alone. He's not the one at fault here."

"What the hell are you talking about? He walked away when you told him you were pregnant with Samantha. He didn't care enough to stay here and raise his child and take care of his responsibilities." He snapped his fingers with an almost maniacal smile lifting his lips. "Wait! I know. I'm going to call Justin and Cole and all three of us will kill him together."

"Damn it, listen to me. Leave him alone. This isn't his fault."

"Why? He needs to take care of his responsibility – his daughter."

"He didn't leave because he wanted to. He left because I told him to." *There. It's out.* The heavy burden she carried with her for nine years finally reared its ugly head.

"What the hell are you saying? You told him to leave?"

She sighed heavily and sank down onto the patio chair. "Yes. I told him to leave. I was seventeen and scared. He was twenty years old, trying to get through college and when I found out about my pregnancy, I didn't know what to do. I couldn't ask him to drop out of school to take care of me and the baby. It wasn't fair to him."

Chase sat down next to her and took her hand in his. "What about you? It wasn't fair for you to have to raise her by yourself."

"No, I guess it wasn't, but I had you, Justin, Cole and Mom and Dad to help me. I knew I could count on my family."

"So he took the easy way out and left town."

"I guess you could say that, yes. He didn't want to. I told him I wouldn't see him anymore. I forced him to leave."

"God, what a mess this is," he said with a heavy sigh.

"This isn't your fight anymore. It's mine and mine alone. I chose the path I took and now that he is back in town, I have to face the choice I made. It changed both our lives and Samantha's. This is my mess to clean up."

"Not alone. You are never alone and you know that."

Tears burned the back of her eyelids when she touched his face. "I love you, Chase, but I have to take care of this myself. I'm not sure how I'm going to fix this, but I will – somehow I will."

* * * *

Wyatt sighed when he sat down on the twin bed in the physician's room to change his shoes. *I'm so glad today is finally over.* Coming face to face with Jamie and his daughter yesterday had taken its toll. All of his dreams last night involved Jamie and he'd slept like shit. Today every patient seemed to take everything out of him.

I knew it would happen eventually. It's not like I could or even wanted to avoid her.

Five fingers cut a path through his hair and then rubbed the back of his neck for a minute. Grabbing his duffle bag, he pulled out his running clothes and changed. Exhaustion tickled the back of his mind, but the restlessness he felt since that afternoon tugged at his insides.

A good run is what I need.

Stretching out the muscles of his legs for several minutes, he pulled open the door and headed for the entrance leading outside.

Feet found a rhythm as they pounded against the pavement. Sweat poured down his back, soaking his t-shirt but he continued to run for over an hour. Ragged breaths rasped from his lungs as his chest heaved with the effort of keeping up the fast past he had set for himself.

Jamie. Jamie. Jamie.

Her name beat against his skull with each footfall hitting the ground beneath him until he stopped and braced his hands on his knees. Sweat dripped into his eyes and he swiped at the salty liquid with his sleeve.

When she had thrown herself into his arms it felt like heaven had opened up and smiled on him again after all these years.

God, I've missed her.

Medical school had been a bitch, but leaving her here, knowing she carried his child, had torn his heart out of chest. He always knew when he finished school, he would return to Laramie. Whether she would let him back in her life, he didn't know.

The day she broke the news surfaced in his mind as he turned around and headed back to the hospital.

"Wyatt. We need to talk."

Burying his nose in the crook of her neck, he nuzzled against it before he ran his tongue up the silky column of skin. A low purr rumbled in her throat for a moment as she tipped her head and gave him better access.

Her voice dropped to a whisper and he smiled against her skin. "We need to talk. I need to tell you something."

"Mmm…whatever it is, it can wait. I need to make love to you." His mouth trailed down her chest and she arched her back as he sucked the pert nipple between his lips. The moan of pleasure from her lips had pride swelling in his heart. Pushing her breast further into his mouth, she fingered the hair at his nape, wrapping the strands around her fingertips.

They had been dating for several months and even though she was only seventeen to his twenty, he knew she had already wound his heart around her little pinky. Her brothers would kill him if they found out they were having sex, but he couldn't seem to help himself with her near. She intoxicated him with her scent, the first time she had walked by him at the pizza parlor and when she flashed those gorgeous dimples, he nearly dropped to her feet and kissed her toes.

"Open for me, baby."

"God, I love when you do that."

Swiping his tongue over the skin of her stomach, he moved lower, toward the warm center that awaited him, skimming the silky flesh and leaving goose bumps in his wake. She parted her slim thighs when his broad shoulders filled the space. When his tongue speared her vagina, she lifted her hips and begged for more. Licking from vagina to clit in one long stroke almost sent her careening over the edge as she whimpered her need above him. Her thighs quivered when he toggled the hardened little nub beneath his tongue until she screamed his name and flooded his mouth with her sweet cum.

He kissed his way back to her lips, slanting his over hers and delving his tongue into her mouth as his stiff cock slipped inside her waiting heat. Gorgeous legs wrapped around his hips, lifting her butt higher as he groaned into her mouth. His lips left hers and his breathing hitched in his throat. Her vagina squeezed him like a vice, almost making him loose control. "God, Jamie. You feel amazing wrapped around me."

"Fuck me, Wyatt, fuck me hard."

He brought her legs up to where they draped across his bulging biceps and his groin slammed into hers. The rocking of his pelvis brought them both to the brink and pushed them over together as her cries of pleasure echoed in his ears.

When the shudders calmed, he released her legs and draped himself over her chest, his nose buried in the crook of her neck. Her fingers skimmed down his back, tickling the skin beneath them. Shifting slightly, he moved to relieve her of his weight, but she held on tight and whispered, "Don't move yet."

"I'll squish you."

"It's okay. I want to feel close to you," she murmured, a small catch in her voice.

After a moment, he lifted his head and brushed the brown curls from her forehead. He frowned when he looked into her eyes and found tears glistening on her lashes. "What's wrong, baby? I didn't hurt you, did I?

"No, you didn't hurt me. You wouldn't ever do that, I know."

"Then what? Why are you crying?"

She shifted under him, forcing him to move from on top of her and sat up on the side of the bed. The clothes on the floor were grabbed and she slipped on her shirt before shimmied into her jeans without a word.

"Jamie, honey. Come on. Tell me what's wrong?"

"I need to tell you something, Wyatt. I tried before we—before we…"

"Before we made love?"

"Yeah, but as usual, you distracted me." Her brown eyes found his and terror gripped his heart. "Put some clothes on, please."

Not liking the look in her eyes, he stood up and reached for his pants before he slipped them on, and then took a seat on the bed again. The soft shuffle of her footsteps across the carpet, sounded loud in the room. "Jamie, sweetheart—whatever it is, we'll work it out together. You know that."

Air rushed from between her lips as she sighed heavily and took several steps away from him before she started to talk. "Wyatt, I know you are only a few years into your college degree and you still have several more to go so you can practice medicine."

"Yeah."

"Please, let me talk." She chewed her bottom lip for a moment before she continued. "I care about you—a lot, but you can't give up your career for me."

"What are you saying, Jamie?" He frowned as confusion raced across his brain. "I'm not giving up anything."

"You will, though. I know you well enough to know that."

"I'm confused, baby. What's going on?"

Facing the window, she blurted out, "Wyatt—I'm going to have a baby—your baby."

He jumped to his feet and almost shouted, "What? You can't be serious. You're on birth control."

"I realize that."

"How can you be pregnant?"

"Come on, Wyatt. You know as well as I do, the pill isn't perfect and we didn't use a condom for the last few months since we were dating exclusively."

Footsteps took the same path she'd make through the carpet. "Pregnant? Shit!" He stopped in front of her and took her shoulders in his hands. "We'll just get married then, and raise this baby together."

She pulled away from him and moved several feet away. "I'm not marrying you."

What the hell? Did she just say she wouldn't marry me?

"Wait! What did you say?"

"I'm not marrying you." She folded her arms under her breasts and her lips pulled into a firm line when the infamous stubborn Wilder streak reared its ugly head.

"But we have to. This is our baby and we'll raise it together like parents should. I'll drop out of school and get a different job."

"No. You are going to stay in school and I'll raise this baby myself with the help of my family. You are not giving up your dream of becoming a doctor because I'm pregnant."

"Fuck! Your brothers are going to kill me! They don't even know we've been having sex, and now this."

A frown pulled down the corners of her mouth as she bit her lower lip. "I hadn't thought of that."

"They will never allow you to raise this baby alone, if they have anything to say about it. What about your parents?"

"It doesn't matter. This is my life and I'll decide what happens, not them. I'm not going to allow you to drop out of school." Worried eyes met his. "Can you transfer somewhere? You can't stay here, Wyatt. They'll kill us both."

"But I love you, Jamie. I don't want to leave town."

Presenting him with her back, she stared out the window for a moment, before she whispered, "I don't love you. I'll carry this baby and raise it alone, but you need to move on—finish school and be the best damned doctor this country has ever seen."

He stepped behind her and grasped her shoulders in his hands. "You're lying. I know you love me."

Inhaling a big breath, she stepped out of his reach before she turned around and her eyes bored into his. "No Wyatt, I don't." She slipped on her flip flops, grabbed her purse and walk out without another word.

Chapter Three

The hot stream of water pricked his skin like tiny needles. Nine years. Nine fucking years he had been without her.

He did as she asked back then. He had been scared; terrified in fact, when she told him she was going to have his baby. For days after their conversation, he had tried to talk to her, but she refused to even see him. Messages went unanswered and going by her house proved to be futile. He had been at a loss as to what to do. Leaving town was the last thing he wanted to do, but he hadn't seen any other choice so he wrote her a letter, mailed it to the house and left.

Walking away from Jamie and his daughter had been the hardest thing he ever had to do—until today. Now, continuing to live in the same town and not touch her would be the harder still.

Maybe she'll let me be a part of her life.

"Yeah, and maybe hell will freeze over tomorrow," he grumbled as he turned off the water and grabbed the towel hanging from the rack next to the stall. Once he dried off, he wrapped it around his lean hips, tucking the end in at his waist before he padded out to the small sleeping room.

Slipping a t-shirt over his head and pulling on his jeans, he jammed his feet into his boots, and ran a comb through his wet hair.

I need a cold beer.

Grabbing his duffle, he pulled open the door and came face to face with Amy.

"Oh, hi, doc. I wondered if you were still here."

He cocked an eyebrow as a flirty smile rippled across her mouth. "Something I can do for you?"

Her green eyes wandered down his frame before coming back to his face. She didn't even try to mask the interest in her gaze. "Mmm…maybe."

A dry chuckle left his mouth. "I mean patient wise."

Her eyes returned to his when she boldly ran a fingernail down his chest.

Damn! Did she ever give up?

"No, but I'm sure I could probably help you."

Two steps to the side and he scooted past her. "Sorry. I'm headed out. I guess I'll see you tomorrow."

With a pouty turn of her lip, she said, "Yeah. I'll be here."

"Night, Amy."

"Night, Wyatt."

He left her standing in the hall as he hit the exit button where his Harley sat in the parking lot. Slipping on his helmet, he straddled the heavy bike before he brought the kickstand up and hit the ignition. With a low growl, the motorcycle turned over and he slowly pulled out into traffic, headed for Cowboy Lights.

Cars and trucks sat packed in the parking lot like sardines in a can. Lucky for him, they kept a smaller area for motorcycles. He swung the bike into a spot, switched it off and pushed the kickstand down. Slipping his helmet into the backpack he carried, he headed for the entrance and the cold beer waiting for him.

Men and women dressed to the hilt in their cowboy garb spilled out onto the long wooden porch. A few faces he recognized and even acknowledge when his name reached his ear on the breeze, but he didn't stop, only raise his hand in greeting. Once inside, the bright lights of the dance floor illuminated the couples twirling to the music from the band on the stage, but he didn't come for the atmosphere.

Raising his hand when he approached the bar, he motioned for the bartender. "Hey, John. Can I leave this back there?"

"Hey, Wyatt." The bartender motioned for Wyatt to hand over his backpack, placed it under the bar and laid a napkin on the glistening bar. "I haven't seen you in a while."

"I know. I've been working a lot. Not much leisure time these days."

"I'm sure they're keeping you busy at the hospital."

Wyatt shook his head and said, "Don't you know it."

"What can I get you?"

"An MGD please."

"No problem." John grabbed a bottle from the cooler to his left, popped the cap and handed it to Wyatt. "Hey—how's that cute little nurse out there? Amy, I think is her name."

Tipping the bottle to his lips, he took a long drag on the longneck before he sat it back on the bar. "Good, I guess. I just saw her a little while ago."

"I wouldn't mind gettin' her number, I tell ya."

A light chuckle left his lips. "I'll see what I can do for you, my friend. She doesn't seem to get that I'm not interested, so maybe if I swing her your way, she'll leave me alone."

John cocked a questioning eyebrow before he said, "You ain't interested? That's kind of surprising."

"Why? She's not my type."

With a quick glance over Wyatt's shoulder, he nodded his head and said, "No, but I know who is."

Glancing in the mirror over the bar, Wyatt realized where John's attention had been drawn to. His heart slammed against his ribs and his breathing hitched in his throat when his gaze found the three women sitting in the corner booth. The sexy brown-haired woman who haunted his dreams sat with two of her friends.

Taking advantage of the fact that Jaime didn't see him standing at the bar, he watched her absently peeled the label off the bottle in her hand. The other two women seemed to be in an animated conversation about something or another, but she appeared to be totally bored. Her gaze scanned the crowd around her, but never rested on anyone in particular for any length of time.

A moment later, a tall blonde cowboy approached the table and she smiled up at the guy, her gorgeous dimples peeking out of her cheeks. Wyatt's gut clenched when she nodded and stood, apparently planning on dancing with the cowboy. She followed the guy onto the dance floor while Wyatt tipped the beer to his lips and took a long pull. He wiped the drop of liquid clinging to his lower lip, as the guy wrapped his arms around her petite waist, his palms settle familiarly on her hips.

Damn it!

Turning toward the music and lights, his gaze found the couple again when he leaned back and rested his elbows on the bar behind him.

Why the hell am I torturing myself this way? Just turn around and forget the fact that the guy is practically seducing her right there on the dance floor.

Anger swept down his spine like a lightning bolt clear to his toes as the cowboy slid his hands across her lower back and then down to her ass cheeks.

He growled low in his throat and pushed away from the bar. Twenty steps and he stood next to them.

"I'm cuttin' in."

The guy's eyes ricocheted to his and Jamie gasped before she stepped out of his embrace.

"Wyatt," she said when she faced him.

"Butt out buddy. She's mine."

"Like hell she is."

"Wyatt—Jake." She placed one hand on each of the two men's chests in a vain attempt to keep them apart, stepping between them. "Just stop this."

Wyatt continued to dare Jake with his gaze, his hands balled into fists at his sides. The other man probably outweighed him by fifty pounds, with biceps that bulged under the strain of keeping his temper in check. If Jake decided to hit him, it wouldn't be a pretty fight, but he wasn't about to back down.

She's mine, damn it!

"Tell him, Jamie," Wyatt growled.

"I'm not telling him anything, Wyatt. This is nuts." With her back plastered against Jake's chest, she held out her hands toward Wyatt, her gaze pleading.

"You're going to allow him to practically fuck you on the dance floor?"

"We were only dancing, nothing more."

"He had his hands on your ass!" he spat.

"It's none of your business."

"The hell it's not!"

"It's not. You know nothing about me anymore."

"Well, if you've changed that much in the last nine years, maybe I don't want to."

She gasped, hurt reflected in her eyes.

"Never mind. Just forget it." He spun on his heels and headed for the bar. Throwing some money down before asking John for his backpack, he headed for the door without a backward glance, cussing in his head all the way out. *Fuck. Fuck. Fuck.* The wooden panel gave way to the pressure of his hand as a blast of warm air hit his face and ruffled his hair. He jumped off the porch, his boots crunching the gravel beneath them when he stomped toward his bike.

Son of a bitch!

Suppressing the urge to throw his backpack across the parking lot in a fit of rage, he pulled out his helmet and slipped the backpack over the back of the bike.

"Wyatt," she said, touching his arm.

He spun around to find Jamie standing behind him. Before he could stop himself, he wrapped his hand in her hair and yanked her up against his chest. His lips came crashing down on hers in a desperate kiss.

She whimpered slightly under the crush of his mouth, but her lips softened under his and she returned the pressure. She opened to the urging of his tongue, wrapping her hands around his neck.

God, she tastes like heaven.

After several moments, he ripped his mouth from hers and opened his eyes as his chest heaved from every ragged breath he tried to pull into his air starved lungs. "Why do you torture me like this?"

"I'm not…"

Pressing his finger against her lips, he effectively silenced her protest. "All you have to do is be in the same room with me to torture me." One finger swept across her bottom lip. "I want nothing more than to fuck you until you scream my name like you used to." The shiver rolling over her body made him smile, as he watched her eyes close.

When she opened them again, her brown eyes danced with fire barely banked and she whispered, "What's stopping you?"

He exhaled on a chuckle. "You." He dropped his arms from around her and stepped back. "I'm not going to take advantage of your momentary loss of control or whatever you want to call it. I want you more than anything I've ever wanted in my life, but it will be when you come to me and want the same thing." Letting his gaze skim her face, a small smile lifted the corners of his mouth before turning back to his bike, straddling the leather seat and hitting the ignition. Without looking at her again, he slipped his helmet on, lifted the kickstand and left her standing there in the middle of the gravel.

* * * *

He pulled out of the driveway and disappeared. She lifted her fingers to her lips where they still tingled from the pressure of his. Her eyes closed and she sighed heavily.

Damn it! Why did he have to come back?

She kicked at the gravel beneath her boot before she stomped back toward the bar. Pushing the heavy door open, she made her way back to the corner table she shared with Candy and Liz.

"Where the hell did you go?"

"Outside."

"Chasing Wyatt?" Liz asked, her eyebrow rising in question.

"Go to hell, Liz," Jamie grumbled as she slid into the booth.

"When are you going to just admit you never got over him?" Candy asked.

"Never."

Liz rolled her eyes. "Good lord, Jamie. Everyone in the bar saw that scene on the dance floor and then you take off after him when he stomps out of here? It's as obvious as the nose on your face."

"I don't care, Liz. There is nothing between me and Wyatt anymore."

"Nothing except the fact that you share a child," Candy said as Jamie gasped. "What? You act like people around here don't know Samantha is his?"

Jamie's jaw dropped. *Is it that obvious?*

"Oh, come on, Jamie," Liz said. "She may have your hair and dimples, but she's got Wyatt's eyes and he disappears from town shortly after you found out you were pregnant. Everyone knew you two were seeing each other pretty seriously."

"It doesn't matter." Jamie shrugged, trying to forget about the kiss they had shared in the parking lot.

"Hey, sweet thing," Jake said, approaching the table next to Jamie. "Shall we finish what we started?"

She cocked her head to the side as her gaze raked him from the top of his blond hair to the tips of his cowboy boots.

He is cute. Built and bulging in all the right places, but he is also so stuck on himself, he wouldn't even know how to please a woman.

"No thanks, Jake."

"Why the hell not?" He put his hands on his hips and his lip stuck out like he was pouting and she almost laughed out loud.

"I'm not interested in what you have to offer. It's as simple as that."

"You know what you are, Jamie Wilder? You are a fucking tease."

Her temper flared and she stood up, going toe-to-toe with the man who stood at least six inches taller than she did. "And you know what you are, Jake Black? You are a fucking moron. You think all you need is that three inch piece of meat between your legs and a few pretty words and all the women will fall at your feet. Well, let me tell you something. I would rather have thirty seconds with Wyatt Crossland than a lifetime with that stubby thing you call a cock." She stood up on the seat behind her and shouted to the crowd gathering around them. "Girl's, trust me when I say it ain't worth it." The women chuckled and the men laughed behind their hands at Jake's expense.

"How would you know, Jamie Wilder? I haven't been able to get you in the sack in over nine years."

The crowd roared with laughter.

"I rest my case."

Jake's complexion flushed crimson when he realized what his words sounded like. He got right in her face and growled, "You bitch! You'll pay for that." Spinning on his heels, he disappeared into the crowd as the roaring laughter followed him.

She got down off the chair and slipped back into the booth with her friends while the crowd dispersed back to their own devices.

"That was hilarious!" Liz exclaimed, continuing to chuckle.

"I think you've made an enemy, Jamie," Candy said.

"Oh well. I didn't like him anyway."

"Then why did you dance with him?"

"Because he asked." Her shoulder lifted in a half shrug. "And I was bored."

"And you didn't know Wyatt was here," Candy interjected.

Jamie frowned and looked down at the scarred tabletop under her hand as she traced a gouge with her finger.

"Why don't you just admit it to yourself and him that you still love him?" Liz asked.

"I never loved him, Liz."

"You are such a liar. I don't know why he left when you found out you were pregnant, but he's back now and obviously still interested in you, if the scene out there meant anything. He would have gone one on one with Jake over you. Most guys wouldn't do that unless they care."

After several minutes, Jamie reached over and grabbed her purse.

"Where are you going? The night is still young," Candy asked.

She slipped out of the booth and stood. "I'm going home. I'll see y'all later."

"Sure. Call me next week and we'll see what kind of trouble we can find."

Jamie rolled her eyes and turned toward the door. Several people stopped her on the way out and jokingly slapped her on the back for putting Jake Black in his place. She just grinned, shook her head and kept going until the warm night air greeted her when she stepped outside. As she walked toward her truck, her gaze found the spot where Wyatt had parked his motorcycle and she remembered the pressure of his mouth. She opened her truck and slid into the cab and slipped the key into the ignition. Laying her head against the steering wheel, she closed her eyes for a moment as her brain battled with her heart. After several moments, she sighed, started the truck, and slipped it into reverse before she backed out of the parking spot.

The lights of Laramie glared brightly on the semi-deserted pavement in front of her when she drove in the opposite direction of her parent's house. After the trip to the emergency room yesterday and running into Wyatt there, she looked up his address. They really needed to talk and she figured now seemed like a good time to her.

What will happen when we are alone?

She shook her head and tried to forget about how he made her body crave his with nothing more than a kiss. "I can't think of that right now. We need to discuss what happens from here. I need to know what he is going to want from me as far as Samantha goes. Hell! She doesn't even know who her father is! How in the hell am I going to explain this to her?"

Turning left onto Quarterhorse Drive, she squinted as she tried to read the addresses until she realized the one she sought obviously sat on the corner. His Harley was in the driveway.

Inhaling sharply, her gaze skimmed over the large house. The lights shone brightly out the front window of the house, when she noticed the lack of curtains on the living room windows and smiled. He never had been one for decorations. His apartment when he was in school hardly had a stick of furniture except the bed they shared on so many occasions. Closing her eyes to the pain in her heart, she felt hot tears burn the back of her eyelids for a moment. It had been the hardest thing she had ever had to do, the day she told him she didn't love him and walked away. He had come by several times for days after that, but she couldn't see him. She would never have been able to let him walk away again if she had seen him, so she locked herself in her room and refused to come out until he had left town. Now he was back and she didn't know how she would be able to handle him being so close, but she knew she had to figure it out. He had a right to know his daughter, she supposed. After all, it wasn't his choice to leave.

She walked up to the front and raised her hand to knock, but hesitated for a moment, biting her lip. Taking a deep breath, she rapped a couple of times and waited.

"I'm coming," she heard him shout from somewhere off in the distance, but as soon as he opened the door her heart slammed against her ribs. Pressure built between her legs and she had to shift slightly in a vain attempt to relieve it while she swallowed, *hard*.

Holy hot damn! I'm in trouble now!

Chapter Four

Wyatt stood leaning against the doorjamb with his shoulder while she surveyed his bare chest. He cocked his head slightly to the side when her gaze traveled down the smattering of chest hair to his belly button and the thin line that disappeared at the waistband of his jeans. He cleared his throat and her gaze ricocheted back to his face. Heat crawl up her neck and splash across her cheeks.

He crossed his arms over the tempting flesh of his broad chest and said, "Something I can do for you?"

"Well…" Her voice squeaked and she had to clear her throat and try again. "I thought we should talk."

"Talk." The corners of his mouth lifted in a smile that she hadn't seen in a very long time—one that could curl her toes in her boots, just like it was right now.

"Yeah. I mean we haven't had a chance to talk and I think we need to get some things straightened out."

His arm swept to the side. "By all means, come on in then so we can…talk."

She frowned for a moment before she stepped over the threshold and moved to walk past him. The scent of his cologne and male musk sent her desire into a raging inferno and she stutter-stepped slightly when she neared him.

Damn it! This is going to be harder than I thought.

"Have a seat." He motioned toward the couch. "Can I get you something to drink?"

"No thanks." She gingerly took a seat on the leather sofa and slid her hands between her knees to try to stop them from shaking when he took the seat next to her. "You have no idea how hard this is for me, Wyatt."

"You don't think it was hard on me when you forced me to leave nine years ago?"

A tear formed at the corner of her eye and she brushed it away with her fingertips, but she couldn't look at him. She didn't want to see the pain on his face—the pain she put there. "I did what I thought would be the best thing for all involved."

"The best thing for whom? It sure in the hell wasn't the best thing for me."

"I did it for you, so you wouldn't drop out of school."

"Me? You didn't even ask me what I wanted. All you thought about was yourself. You didn't give a shit about me or the daughter you carried in your belly—my daughter." He jumped to his feet and started to pace as he raked his fingers through his hair. "I don't even know her. God! She's nine years old and I don't even know her at all. I'm assuming by the complete lack of recognition on her part, she doesn't know who I am."

"No."

"What the fuck did you tell her? That I left you? That I died?"

The pain in his eyes sliced her heart to ribbons and she rubbed the spot on her chest right above where the shattering organ lay. "It hasn't come up in conversation yet. She's just started asking about you lately. Up until now, she just accepted things the way they were."

Head tipped back on his shoulders, he said, "You realize I want to be a father to her."

"I know," she whispered and a tear slipped down her cheek. "I know it won't make up for what happened, but I'm sorry. I don't know what else to say."

Turquoise eyes leveled on her. "Has anyone else been raising my daughter?"

She chuckled dryly as she wiped the remaining tears from her cheeks. "You've got to be kidding me? No one, but Chase. I can't even go out anywhere without every man in this town avoiding me like the plague. The reputation of the overprotective Wilder brothers precedes me everywhere I go."

"Well, good 'ole Jake certainly seemed willing to take on the Wilder brothers to get into those skin tight jeans."

Anger zipped through her as she stopped in front of him and squared her shoulders. "Fuck you, Wyatt."

"Not until you beg me," he growled seconds before his arm snaked around her waist and he yanked her to his chest. She managed to bring her hands up, but his quick action just flattened her palms against the soft hair as it tickled her fingertips.

Her unflinching gaze met his and their rasping breaths mingled in the small space separating their lips. With a tortured snarl, his mouth came down on hers, slanting across lips while his hand fisted in her hair. She whimpered but gave into the sensations he created. Opening for him, she accepted his tongue, entangling it with her own.

Good lord, it's been way too long since I've felt like this. "Nine years," her heart whispered as she slipped her hands up around his neck and tangled her fingers in the hair at his nape.

Lips skimmed across her cheek to her ear until his teeth found her sensitive earlobe, nipping softly when she tipped her head to the side. He moved his hand from her back to her breast and cupped it with his palm, his thumb brushing the nipple until it hardened under his touch. Arching toward him, she pushed her breast further into his hand. Her breath hitched in her throat as a moan bubbled in her chest. He nibbled her neck, forcing a whimper from her mouth. The rough pad of his tongue soothed the sting of his teeth moments before he moved back toward her ear. One jean clad thigh slipped between hers and he forced her groin closer to his with a palm against her lower back.

"Tell me you want this as much as I do, baby."

"Oh God yes," she whispered as she gave into the desire racing out of control between them. It had always been like this when they made love. The fire raging between them, simmered under the surface. Even when they were dating, her need for him bordered on out of control.

Both of his hands slipped around and cupped her ass before he lifted her into this arms and she wrapped her legs around his waist. The pulse at the base of his throat raced and she licked the spot, eliciting a groan from deep inside him. His heart raced in time with hers and the thought thrilled her. Stepping back toward the leather couch, he went down with her as they sprawled across the cool surface in a tangle of arms and legs. One hand moved under her shirt, pushing it up along with her bra until his palm found her breast. The hard nub puckered under his fingers as he rolled it between his thumb and finger.

His slick tongue dove inside the cavern of her mouth, licking and stroking along hers, like she knew he would do to her clit if she asked. Her pussy clenched and her pussy wept with need at the thought. Fingers skimmed down, across her stomach until they reached the snap at her waist and plucked it free with deft practice.

Lips brushed against her cheek once he tore them away. The wet slide of his tongue found her ear moments later, before sliding down her neck to the spot where her shoulder and collarbone met. He laved at the spot as his fingers slid through the curls beneath his hand. Opening her thighs, she begged for his touch with soft whimpers. Cream wept from her pussy and she groaned her pleasure when one finger brushed her clit before it slipped knuckle deep into her waiting flesh. Her back arched and she clutched his head, pushing him harder against her when he sucked her nipple.

She whimpered at the loss when the finger disappeared from her aching center and he chuckled softly against her skin.

Damn him! He knows exactly what he's doing to me.

Her hips wiggled and lifted when he grabbed the waistband of her jeans and slipped them off before he tossed them, along with her underwear, across the room.

His mouth moved from her breast, down her stomach and stopped at her belly button. "When did you get this?" His tongue flicked at the dangling belly button ring.

"A few years ago."

"It's sexy as hell," he whispered against her skin before he moved further down. "Open for me, baby."

Her thighs parted and she almost screamed when his warm breath flittered across her aching center. When his tongue licked from vagina to clit, she groaned and tossed her head from side to side and clutched the cool leather beneath her palms. After only a few swipes of his tongue, her body clenched as her climax rolled over her. His name ripped from her throat in the throes of her passion.

He kissed his way back up her stomach once the roar of ecstasy passed, stopping to lick her nipple for a moment before he found his way back to her mouth. His tongue dipped between her lips as she felt the nudge of his cock against her pussy. Somehow during her throes of ecstasy, he had managed to shed his jeans, slip on a condom and now waited for her to accept him inside her aching core.

He tore his mouth away and pressed his forehead against hers, his chest heaving with every breath he took.

She opened her eyes to see him watching her, his gaze burning with carefully controlled desire.

"Tell me."

Uneven breaths tore air from her lungs while she tried to decide whether to fight the fire racing through her veins. She didn't want to ache for him like this, but she did. No one in the last nine years had been able to tap into the smoldering need inside her, the way he had.

"Tell me, Jamie, or I walk away right now."

Her lips parted, but the words wouldn't come.

With a heavy sigh, he pushed away from her. Before he could move completely off, she grabbed his biceps and planted her lips against the rapidly beating pulse at the base of his neck. She sucked the skin into her mouth and heard him groan above her. Licking his neck until she could reach his ear, she whispered, "Fuck me. I need you. Make me come again and scream your name like you used to." She wrapped her legs around his hips and planted her heels against his buttocks, encouraging him to slide inside. "Please, Wyatt."

With a tortured groan, he followed her back down on the sofa. His cock filled her with one motion of his hips, stretching her to accommodate his size. When his heat penetrated her, she groaned softly against the skin of his neck

He didn't move for a moment, just seemed content to be inside her until she wiggled her hips and locked her heels behind him. When his hips started to rock, her pussy clenched and spilled her need on the couch beneath her.

His lips found the shell of her ear and he whispered, "God, you feel good."

A whimper left her lips and she lifted her hips, spurring him on the only way she could without giving up her heart. He lifted his chest and he locked his gaze on her face as his groin met hers. Reaching around behind him and grabbing her legs, he draped them over his forearms before he pushed inside her so deep, she almost climaxed with the one thrust.

"I can feel you gathering. Your pussy is rippling around my cock." He pumped inside her several more times, growling his own pleasure deep and low in his throat before he murmured, "Come for me, baby."

His words ripped apart her control as his name spilled from between her lips and her own came from him on a growl. He shuttered above her and dropped her legs before he collapsed across her chest. Fingertips skimmed down his back and she smiled when his skin quivered under her touch. Hot breath rasped against her neck while his hand slipped up her side and then cupped her breast in his palm.

The compatible silence broke with the ring of her cell phone. He lifted his head and their eyes met while the questions raced across her mind—questions she wasn't sure she wanted to answer. "I need to see who that is. It could be Chase or my mom."

They both groaned when he slipped from her warmth. He sat up and she moved to grab her purse off the other end of the couch.

"Hello?"

"Jamie? Where are you?"

A sigh rushed from between her lips. "I'm out, Mom. Why?"

"It's Samantha. She's running a fever and her broken arm is warm to touch. She is also complaining it hurts really badly."

"How high is her fever?" Jamie asked as worry laced her voice.

"One hundred and three." She heard her mother sigh on the other end of the phone line. "I think you need to come home."

"Shit." Rubbing her forehead for a moment, she said, "All right. I'll be home in a little bit."

"What's wrong?" Wyatt asked, sitting back on the couch next to her.

"It's Sam," she told him as she heard her mother say on the other end of the phone, "Who is that, Jamie?"

"Never mind, Mom. I'll be home in as soon as I can." She closed the phone with a click and stood up before she searched for her jeans. Wyatt dangled them from his fingertips along with her underwear and she felt heat creep up her neck. "Thanks."

"I'm coming with you."

Her gaze flew up to his and she shook her head in denial. "I don't think that is a good idea, Wyatt."

"If she is sick, maybe I need to look at her. Your mom said she was running a fever?"

She chewed her bottom lip nervously while she straightened her clothes.

What if she is really sick? He could help her. He is a doctor after all and her father, even if she doesn't know that.

"Yeah, a hundred and three."

"She could have some kind of infection with the break in her arm." He waited, giving her the choice as to whether he would be welcome to come along or not. The tone gave her the impression he would check on Samantha one way or another.

"All right—fine. You can follow me back to my Mom's."

A smile rippled across his lips and she felt like slapping him as she grumbled under her breath about 'stubborn men.'

He stood and headed toward what she assumed to be his bedroom. Several moments later, he returned with a black t-shirt stretched enticingly across his broad chest, jeans and boots.

"Ready?"

Without saying a word, she grabbed her purse and headed for the door. He pulled it closed behind them and locked it as she walked toward where her truck sat parked against the curb. She watched him straddle his Harley and sighed when she remembered those firm thighs and tight ass between hers legs, a short time ago.

"Enough, Jamie," she chastised herself before she slipped into the cab of her truck. Once she had started her vehicle, she looked into the rearview mirror and pulled away from the curb, keeping Wyatt in her sights. "This is a bad idea. I just know something terrible is going to happen with him coming over. Why the hell did I agree to this?" The reprimands continued until she pulled into her parent's driveway. She wasn't sure how she would explain his presence to her mother and father or how they would react to him.

Her head whipped around when the door popped open and he held it open for her. She hadn't even heard him stop the motorcycle.

She slipped out of the truck and slammed it shut before she headed for the front porch with him on her heels. Her father stood behind the screen and pushed it open the screen when they approached and she could read the confusion on his face.

"Dad—you know Wyatt."

"Uh...of course. Come on in. It's been a long time."

"It certainly has," Wyatt replied, grasping the screen and holding it for her to precede him into the house.

"I didn't realize you were back in town, son."

"I haven't been for long. A couple of months or so is all."

They walked into the living room and her mother gasped in surprise. "Wyatt?

"Hi, Mrs. Wilder."

"My goodness! Where have you been? It's been ages since we've seen you, young man."

Jamie caught his gaze and the questioning raise of his eyebrow. *I need to let him in on some of mom's memory loss and mild dementia that came with her stroke the year before.*

"I moved to California to finish my medical degree, but I came back here to practice."

"Mom, Wyatt is the one who treated Samantha at the emergency room the other day and set her arm."

"But…"

"No, Mom, Samantha doesn't know."

"But, Jamie…"

"Mom—let it be for now." With a heavy sigh, she and fought the urge to lean into the warm embrace of the devastatingly handsome man who stood near her back. "Where's Sam?"

"In her room."

She moved toward the stairs, but stopped and looked over her shoulder at Wyatt as he continued to stand where he was. "Are you coming?"

"Yeah."

They walked up the stairs together and she stopped at her daughter's bedroom and knocked softly. "Sammy?"

"Mom?" Jamie heard when she pushed it open.

"Yeah, baby," she murmured, moving to the side of Samantha's bed and sitting down on the edge. "How do you feel?" She brushed the sticky hair away from her daughter's forehead.

"I don't feel very good, Mom."

"I know, sweetie." Her worried eyes met Wyatt's. "She's burning up."

He bent down by the bed and smiled softly. "Hi, pumpkin." His hand moved over the area above the cast on her arm and he frowned.

"Hi, Wyatt. What are you doing here?"

"Your mom said you weren't feeling good so I thought I would come by and see you." He looked at Jamie. "Find out if your mom gave her any Tylenol or Motrin."

Jamie nodded and rose from the bed, but froze when Samantha whimpered behind her. "It's all right, baby. I'll be right back and Wyatt will stay with you. Okay?"

"Okay."

She stopped and let her gaze slip back to where Wyatt sat on the side of the bed now and held his daughter's hand. He whispered softly to her and pushed the hair back off her forehead. The whole scene broke Jamie's heart and she felt tears choke her throat before she slipped out and headed back downstairs.

When she reached the living room, her parent's stopped their conversation. "Mom, Wyatt wants to know if you gave Sam anything for her fever."

"I gave her some Tylenol about an hour ago. Right before I called you."

Bonnie's concerned eyes rested on her for a moment and she sighed. "Just say it Mom, okay? Whatever you are going to say, I've probably already said to myself, so spit it out."

"Nothing, Jamie. I'm surprised, that's all. I didn't know Wyatt was back in town and I didn't realize you were seeing him."

"I'm not seeing him." *Never mind that you had mind-blowing sex a short time ago.* "I went by his house to talk about Samantha."

"I see."

"Just stop. Don't read anything into this. He is here because he's concerned about Sam." She turned on her heel and headed back up the stairs. When she reached Samantha's room, Wyatt still sat on the side of her bed. "Mom said she gave her some about an hour ago."

"That should be fine then. We'll keep an eye on her and see if the fever comes down. Why don't you give her some of the pain medication I prescribed? That should help too."

Jamie nodded and moved toward the small bathroom off to her left adjoining her room and Samantha's. Retrieving two of the tablets, she grabbed the glass on the counter to get some water, before she returned to her daughter's bedside. "Here, sweetie. Take these."

Once the pills were swallowed, Samantha sat back on the pillows and looked up at Wyatt in what Jamie could almost describe as hero-worship. "Wyatt?"

"Yeah, pumpkin?"

"Can I ask you a question?"

Jamie's heart began to thump loudly in her chest.

"Sure," Wyatt answered.

"Mom told me something at the hospital the other day and I wanted to ask you about it."

Concerned eyes found Jamie's as she took the chair next to the bed. "Okay."

"Mom said you knew my dad. Can you tell me about him?"

Oh fuck! Wyatt's startled gaze bounced from hers back to Samantha and Jamie said, "Baby, listen…"

"No, Mom. I want to know and you never talk about him. Every time I've asked, you avoid my questions so I decided I had to ask someone else who knew him."

"What has your mom told you?"

"Not much, other than I have his eyes and he was cool, but I don't know what kinds of things he liked, if I look like him, did he do good in school. I don't even know his name."

"I would love to tell you about him, pumpkin, but I think this conversation needs to happen between you and your mother, not me."

Jamie sighed in relief.

"I do think she needs to tell you about him, though. I think it's important for us to know our parents." He stared pointedly at Jamie and her shoulder lifted in a half shrug.

"Mom?"

"You need to rest, Sam. We can talk about this some other time." Jamie tucked the covers up around Samantha's shoulders.

Samantha yawned. "Wyatt, are you and my mom dating?"

He chuckled softly and took his daughter's hand in his. "I don't think I would call it that."

"What would you call it then?"

"We're old friends, sweetheart. Your mom and I knew each other a long time ago."

Another yawn spread her mouth wide. "I think you should date her."

"I'll keep that in mind," he answered with a smile when her eyes drifted shut.

"Is she going to be okay?"

"I think she'll be fine, but she does need to be watched closely. She could have an infection near the break and will possibly need antibiotics. It depends on how she reacts tonight to the Tylenol. If her fever stays down, it could just be a reaction to the break."

Jamie shuffled her feet and her gaze rested on the tips of her boots.

"I think we need to talk about what happened earlier."

She lifted her head and their eyes locked. "I...uh...I'm sorry. It shouldn't have happened—I shouldn't have allowed it to happen."

"Why not?"

"Can we not talk about this right now? Not here, anyway." She looked at Sam, then back to him.

"Fine." He took her hand and led her out into the hall, before he pulled the door shut on their daughter's room. His body pinned her to the wall behind her. "Now—why shouldn't it have happened? I know you wanted me as much as I wanted you."

"It was just a moment of weakness, Wyatt."

His hand slipped into the hair near her ear before it moved around to the back of her head. "A moment of weakness."

"Yeah," she whispered when she felt him draw her closer until his lips were a mere hairsbreadth away. "I had an itch and you were available to scratch it."

He leaned back. "An itch?"

Her shoulder lifted in a shrug.

I can't let him get any closer to tearing down the wall I built around my heart when he left. Yes, she had been the one to tell him to leave, but she had done it for him.

"It's been a while since I've had sex and you still know how to push my buttons. You were available and I took advantage of it."

Dropping his hands, he stepped back farther and frowned. "I didn't realize how much of a heartless bitch you have turned into." Before, his eyes had sparkled with desire, now they shone lifeless and dull as he looked at her. "I'll check on Sam tomorrow. Be warned, I fully intend to tell her who I am by next weekend if you haven't already."

She sucked in a shocked breath and stared. "You wouldn't."

"Yes I would. She's my daughter and I'm done letting you shut me out of her life."

"But…"

"But nothing, Jamie. I will have a relationship with her even if you and I can't stand to be in each other's company anymore."

Anger clouded his face before he spun on his heels and disappeared down the stairs. The front door slammed behind him and she jumped.

Fighting the urge to bang her head against the wall behind her in frustration, she closed her eyes and sighed. *Son of a bitch! Now what the hell am I going to do?*

Chapter Five

Bright and early the following morning, Wyatt stood on the stoop, his Harley at the curb when she answered the bell.

"I came by to see Sam."

"I figured as much. It's not like you are here to see me." She stepped aside and allowed him to enter. "Would you like some coffee? Sam's not awake yet."

"Sure."

"I'll be right back," she said before she headed toward the kitchen. When she reached the countertop near the coffeepot, she stopped to take a few ragged breaths.

Damn it! Why does he have to affect me like this? Just the smell of his freshly washed hair and the hint of his own unique musky scent had her heart hammering against her ribs. Her hands shook when she tried to pour him a cup of coffee and she splashed some of the scalding liquid over her hand. "Son of a bitch!"

"Everything okay?"

"Yes. I just burned my hand."

A moment later, he stood by her side. Grasping her hand in his, he turned it over and inspecting the red skin. He pulled her closer to the sink and turned on the water. "Here. Hold it under the cold water for a minute."

She hissed as the liquid hit her heated skin. "That hurts."

"It's the best thing for a burn. It'll feel better in a minute."

Never mind the fact that his touch is heating up the rest of my body to a boiling temperature.

Capturing her lips between her teeth, she swallowed hard and shifted her glance to his profile for a second. He focused on her hand so she had a chance to study him. Lashes any woman would kill for covered his amazing eyes. The color had always fascinated her from the first moment they'd locked gazes. The bump over the bridge of his nose hadn't been there before and his face seemed slimmer now than it had been at twenty. His lips still held the same fullness and promise of passion. Whiskers shadowed his jaw and a tick appeared when he clenched his teeth.

"Stop looking at me like that, Jamie," he whispered without looking at her.

"Like what?" she murmured.

"Mmm…let's see." He turned slightly and lifted his face, locking his gaze with hers. "Like you want a repeat of last night."

"Maybe I do."

He inhaled sharply and let go of her hand. "You've turned into a real tease."

"I'm not…" Her words were cut off as they heard Samantha yell from upstairs. "I'll be right there, baby." She dried off her hand, before she turned to head back toward the living room and the stairs. Once she reached the bottom, she wasn't surprised to see Wyatt right behind her.

"I think I can handle this, Wyatt. I have been taking pretty good care of her for the last nine years."

"Only because you wouldn't allow me to."

With hands on her hips and legs planted apart, she grumbled, "You knew where we were. It's not like I've moved."

His eyes narrowed into agitated slits. "You aren't pinning this whole thing on me. You forced me out of your life. I didn't have a lot of choice in the matter, if I remember correctly."

"It doesn't matter right now. *My* daughter needs me."

She took two steps up as she heard behind her, "*Our* daughter needs *us*." Sighing heavily, she continued up the stairs until she reached Samantha's bedroom and knocked softly. She pushed open the door and found her daughter sitting up in the bed.

The turquoise blue eyes lit up when they rested on the man behind her. "Wyatt!"

"Hi, pumpkin."

"What are you doing here?"

"I came to check on you again since you weren't feeling too well last night." He moved to the side of the bed and took a seat next to her before he put his hand on her forehead. "Your fever is better, I see."

"I feel a lot better today."

"Good."

Twin sets of blue eyes pinned Jamie where she stood as Samantha said, "Mom? I want to get up."

"I think you need to stay there today."

"But, I feel fine now and I want to show Brandy to Wyatt."

"Brandy?" he asked, shooting Jamie a glance.

"Her mare. The one she fell off of the other day at the rodeo."

His gaze swung back to the little girl. "What were you doing that you fell off? I never got a chance to ask you at the hospital the other day."

"I ride barrels."

"Really? Are you any good?"

Samantha's shoulders pulled back smugly. "Yeah. I'm number two in the area right now."

"Number two, huh?" He smiled proudly as his eyes twinkled.

Samantha frowned. "Yeah. Olivia Aslin is number one, but I'll get by her before the end of the season. How long do I have to wear this thing?" She lifted her still splinted arm.

"Probably about six weeks at least."

"Can I ride with it?"

"You'll have to ask the other doctor that, but my guess is no."

"But, Mom?"

Jamie answered, "We'll have to ask the doctor, baby. If he says no, then it's no. I imagine Wyatt knows what he's talking about since he's a doctor, too."

Samantha stubbornly crossed her arms over her chest as another frown pulled down the corners of her mouth. "Can't you talk to him, Wyatt? If I have to stay in this thing and not be able to ride, I'll lose for sure."

"Well don't jump to conclusions until you talk to him and he can see the pictures I had taken the other day, okay?"

"All right. I guess I don't have much choice, huh."

A soft chuckle left his lips. "Not really, pumpkin."

"I don't want to stay in this bed though, Mom. Can't I get up? Plleeease?" Jamie could rarely tell her daughter no, especially when she pinned her with the eyes that were so much like her father's.

"All right."

"Yes!" Samantha flipped the covers back and jumped from the bed in one swift motion.

"But, you aren't doing anything heavy today. And you aren't going to Ashley's."

"But…"

Jamie folded her arms across her chest. "No buts young lady. It's all or nothing."

"Okay." Samantha hugged her and Jamie wrapped her arms around her daughter as her eyes met Wyatt's over the little girl's head. Samantha pulled out of her arms and looked up at her. "Can I show Wyatt, Brandy?"

"I guess that would be okay."

Samantha flashed a dimpled smile at Wyatt before she grabbed her clothes and disappeared into the bathroom.

"She's a hand full." Wyatt's amused smile rippled across his face.

"No. Really? How did you guess?"

"Like her mother."

Jamie cocked an eyebrow at the man sitting on the side of the bed, but kept her mouth shut. She didn't want to get into a big discussion with him right now. Samantha might hear something Jamie wasn't ready for her to know.

A moment later, the bathroom panel burst open and Samantha rushed out, dressed and ready. She grabbed Wyatt's hand when she reached his side and pulled him to his feet. "Come on."

Jamie watched as the two of them disappeared. Rubbing her temples for a moment, she felt the beginnings of a headache, and she sighed heavily before she moved to follow.

* * * *

Sunlight reflected brightly off the metal siding on the barn as Wyatt allowed Samantha to lead him outside.

"She's in the stall in the barn."

"Well, let's have a look then. I'm sure she beautiful."

Samantha flashed her dimples at him and he almost forgot to breath. *They are so much like Jamie's, it hurts to see them.*

"You okay?" she asked with a frown.

Shaking his head for a second to clear his thoughts, he said, "I'm fine, pumpkin. You just look so much like your mom when you smile."

She shrugged. "I'm cursed with the Wilder dimples."

"They aren't a curse. Trust me. You'll be wrapping boys around your little finger in no time with those things."

"Really?"

"Yeah, really."

"Do you like mom's?" she asked when they reached the barn.

"That's not a fair question, young lady."

"Why not? I know you like her."

"Do you."

Eyes rolled and she said, "It's obvious, Wyatt. You can't keep your eyes off her when you are in the same room. I don't know why you don't just date her."

"Maybe she doesn't want to date me."

She giggled when they approached the stall where a pretty little chestnut mare poked her head over the wall and Samantha ran her hand over the horse's nose. "Yeah, right. She wants to be with you, too."

He couldn't believe he stood there having this conversation with their daughter while she gave him advice on her mother. "Well, we'll see what happens. I'm not counting my chickens. Your mother can hardly stand to be in the same room with me."

"Whatever, Wyatt. I know my mom better than that. She's got the hots for you."

A roar of laughter burst from his lips he asked, "The hots?"

With a quick nod and a roll of her eyes, she said, "You haven't been around kids very much, huh." She sighed before she continued, "You know—attracted to you—wants to get you in the sack."

"Samantha Renee Wilder!" Jamie exclaimed from the doorway.

Samantha cringed and whispered to Wyatt, "Oops. Busted." She turned and looked at her mother. "Hi, Mom."

"You did not just tell Wyatt I want to get him in the sack."

Samantha shrugged and looked at him, her eyes twinkling with mischief. "Yep."

His gaze rested on the obviously unhappy Jamie as she approached with long strides and he had to laugh. If Samantha only knew what they had done last night, she would realize, at least he had the 'hots' for her mom.

"That's about enough of that talk, young lady."

"Why? It's the truth, isn't it?"

Jamie stopped dead in her tracks and stammered, "Well I…"

"See! You can't even deny it."

"What goes on between me and Wyatt is none of your business, Samantha."

"But I think he would make a cool dad."

"Samantha!"

"Wait just a minute. I think you're getting way ahead of yourself," he said as he slipped his hands in the pocket of his jeans and resisted the urge to pull the girl into a hug.

"I don't see why. You are both attracted to each other."

"More goes into a relationship than just being attracted to someone, Sam. Your mom may already be seeing someone and it's not fair…"

"She's not," Samantha interrupted.

Jamie sighed. "I don't think Wyatt needs to know about other men in my life."

"There aren't any other guys, Mom. You said yourself Uncle Chase won't allow a guy to even look at you."

"We are *not* having this conversation, Samantha Renee."

Samantha leaned toward him and whispered, even though her voice was loud enough he knew Jamie heard her, "She always uses my middle name when she's mad at me."

He chuckled as he got a kick out of Samantha sparring words with Jamie. His daughter definitely had his dry wit. "Ah, yes. The Wilder brother's reputation you mentioned last night."

Jamie flushed bright red and he knew she remembered what happened after that, just like he did. He slid his arm around Samantha's shoulders and pulled her to his side. "I think we need to give your mom a break. We are kind of ganging up on her."

"Nah," Samantha replied.

With a quick glance at Jamie and he asked, "Why don't you let me take you two out for breakfast?"

"Yeah!"

"I don't think…"

"Come on, Mom. If the guy wants to take us out, let him!"

Jamie scowled as her eyes locked on Samantha.

"Please?" The corners of his mouth lifted in a smile and he saw Jamie rub her arms.

"All right, but as soon as we're done, we are coming back here."

"Yeess!" Samantha exclaimed as she slipped away from his side and hugged Jamie.

"We will have to take my truck though. We can't all fit on your bike."

"Bike? What kind of bike?"

"I'll show you. Come on." Samantha and Jamie followed him back toward the house where Jamie grabbed her purse, before they walked out.

"That's yours?" Samantha asked, her voice cracking in awe when they stopped next to his Harley.

"Yep."

"Cool! Can you take me for a ride?"

"Not right now, but maybe when we get back. It's up to your mom, though."

Samantha pleaded with her mother. "Can he, Mom, please?"

"We'll see when we get back."

They climbed into her truck and drove to the local Waffle House out on highway 287. As they got out, he saw several sets of eyes swivel toward them and jaws drop in astonishment.

Damn! I forgot how small this town really is.

"Are you sure about this, Jamie?" he asked with a tip of his head toward the staring patrons.

"It's fine. I don't care what people think—never have. You should know that by now."

He chuckled while he held the door open for the two females with him. "I guess I had forgotten."

They took a booth and he sat across from Jamie and Samantha. The waitress walked up to their table, and with a surprised gasp, she said, "Well, Wyatt Crossland. I didn't realize you were back in town."

"Hi, Andrea. Nice to see you."

"You too, honey." The woman's eyes swept over Jamie and Samantha. "Why, isn't this just a cozy family scene."

"Andrea," he growled in warning, but the woman ignored him.

"I bet you're just enjoying this all to pieces, eh Samantha? How cool is that—to have both your mom and dad having breakfast with you after he's been gone so long."

Samantha's eyes locked with his for a moment before they moved to her mother and then back the waitress. A nervous laugh bubbled from her lips. "Wyatt's not my dad. He's just a friend of mom's."

The waitress looked at Jamie and she gave her a slight shake of her head that he barely caught as her eyes narrowed in warning.

"Yeah—right. Sorry honey. My mistake." She pulled out her ordering pad and said, "What can I get y'all to drink?"

Once they had finished ordering their drinks and food, Samantha excused herself to go to the little girl's room, giving him a chance to say something to Jamie. "We need to talk to her and soon. She's going to find out from someone other than us if we don't, and I'm not sure about you, but I certainly would rather she hear it from us."

"I know," Jamie whispered before she shot a glance over her shoulder.

"Why don't you come over to my place tonight for dinner and we can talk to her."

"I'm not sure that's a good idea."

"We need to tell her."

"Tell her what?" Samantha said when she approached the table.

Jamie turned white. "Uh…"

"Just that your mom agreed to come by my house and have dinner later, just the three of us."

Jamie's eyes narrowed and spit fire at him from across the table, but he only smiled.

"Cool. Can you take me on your bike and mom and follow in the truck?" Samantha asked when she slid back into the booth next to Jamie.

"I'm sure we can arrange something."

They managed to make small talk until they were done eating. Thankfully there were no more episodes like before where Samantha might find out about her parentage, before they could talk to her. Samantha kept the conversation lively as they rode back to Jamie's parents' house.

When they were headed toward the door, Samantha asked, "Are you coming in, Wyatt?"

"It depends on if your mom says it's okay. I don't want to intrude."

"I'm sure it's fine. Come on." She grabbed his hand and pulled him toward the house while Jamie shook her head and frowned.

Once they were inside, he could hear voices coming from the living room and he frowned himself when he heard a familiar voice. The last person he wanted to talk to right now was Jamie's brother. "I think I should go. I have some things to do at the house before you two come over for dinner," he said as he pulled against the grasp of her hand.

"That's crazy, Wyatt. Uncle Chase is here and you said you hadn't talked to him in a long time. I'm sure he'll be happy to see you again."

Oh no, he won't.

Samantha managed to drag him into the living room and his gaze locked on the blue eyes of Jamie's brother. Chase's eyes narrowed into angry slits before he rose from the couch and moved toward Wyatt with the grace of a panther. Chase stopped in front of him, pulled back his fist and hit him square in the jaw, forcing Wyatt back against the front door.

Stars flashed behind Wyatt's eyes and Samantha screamed.

"Uncle Chase, stop!"

He ignored his niece and growled, "You son of a bitch! What the hell are you doing here?"

Chapter Six

Abby appeared by Chase's side in a flash, stepping between her husband and Wyatt. Jamie stood pinned to the wall and Samantha yelled at Chase to stop.

"This doesn't help things, honey," Abby said softly, facing her husband.

"He's the one who ran out, Abby." His eyes locked on his wife for a moment before they returned to Wyatt.

"We had this conversation," Jamie said, stepping closer. "It wasn't his fault. I told you that."

"He could have stayed anyway. He took the chicken-shit way out and left town so he wouldn't have to deal with his responsibilities."

"I didn't have much choice in the matter, Chase. Jamie wouldn't even talk to me," Wyatt explained. "You know your sister."

"Yeah, I do, but what about the last nine years, Wyatt? It's not like you didn't know where she lived."

"I realize that too. I never said this was all her fault. I accept the blame for how things have turned out as well."

"Are you prepared to take responsibility for Samantha now? Are you prepared to be a father to her like you should have been for the last nine years?"

Jamie heard a startled gasp and spun around. All of them had completely forgotten Samantha stood nearby.

"Samantha—baby. Let me explain."

"He's my dad?"

"Sam…"

"Tell me now, Mom. No more lies and no more avoiding the questions. Is Wyatt my father?"

Jamie closed her eyes as the deafening silence filled the space around them. When she opened them again, tears burned her eyes and gathered at the corners. The hurt look on Samantha's face tore her heart to shreds. "Yes, baby, he is."

Samantha looked at Wyatt with the same hurt. "Did you know? Even at the hospital, did you know even then?" Wyatt wiped the blood from his lip and moved toward Samantha, but she stepped back. "Tell me the truth. Did you know even then?"

"Yeah, pumpkin, I did. As soon as I saw your name on the triage sheet, I knew who you were."

Tears streamed down her cheeks as she sobbed. "I don't believe you two! Neither one of you could be honest with me!" She turned on her heel and ran out of the living room. Jamie jumped when the back door slammed. She took a step to follow, but Wyatt stopped her with a hand on her arm.

"Let me. Maybe I can explain."

"But…"

"She's upset, Jamie. Let me try, okay?"

Jamie nodded and watched as he disappeared through the kitchen.

* * * *

The ragged sobs of his daughter sliced his heart like a knife through soft butter. Keeping the secret from her had been wrong, he knew that now. Reaching out to her was the only way he could think of to fix this. Staying away from her for the last nine years had been wrong on his part.

He followed the sounds of her sobs until he stood at the base of the ladder leading to the hayloft above. As he climbed up, the sobs were louder, until his head reached the top and he could see her sitting in the corner on a bale of hay. Curled up in a little ball, her shoulders shook with each ragged sob and each tormented breath.

"Sam?" he whispered, approaching slowly before he sat down next to her.

"Go away, Wyatt."

"Nope. Sorry, pumpkin, but I'm here to stay."

Her teary eyes met his. "Why? You didn't stay before?"

His dejected sigh echoed in the quietness of the barn. The silence was only broken by an occasional whinny of a horse or the stomp of a hoof on dry ground. "I know, and I'm sorry. I took the easy way out back then."

"Why did you leave? Didn't you want me and Mom?"

He wrapped his arm around her shoulder and tucked her to his side. "God, Sammy," he whispered, his own tears threatening to fall down his cheeks. "I wanted you and I wanted your Mom, but I let her convince me the right thing to do was for me to leave and finish school. We were so young. I still had several years of college left so I could practice medicine. She wouldn't let me quit school and take care of her and you. I took the coward's way out, I guess you could say, and left town. I always knew I would come back here once I finished and that's why I'm here now."

"You came back for us?"

He smiled ruefully. "Yeah."

"Do you love Mom?"

"I don't know anymore, Sam. We are different people now than we were back then."

"Did you love her when she got pregnant with me?"

"Yeah, or at least I think I did. It's hard to know at twenty years old."

A frown creased the skin between her eyebrows. "You aren't married or dating someone are you?

He laughed. "No."

Wiping the lingering tears from her cheeks, she said, "Good."

"Good?"

"Yeah. You can't get back together with Mom if you already have a wife."

"Don't get your hopes up, Samantha. I'm not sure your Mom wants that."

One very unladylike snort left her lips as she covered her nose and mouth with her hand. "Do you want to?"

What the hell do I say to that?

"I'm not sure what I want right now, other than to get to know you and spend time with you. I'm sorry I missed being here while you were little. I'm sure you were cute as a button." He tweaked her nose and smiled.

She snuggled next to his side. "I think I'm going to like having you for a Dad." Her eyes met his again and a frown pulled down the corners of her mouth. "What do I call you?"

"You can call me Wyatt or Dad. Whatever you are comfortable with. I know this is going to take some time to get used to. It's kind of weird for me, too."

She straightened up as he looked at her face and a big grin rippled across her mouth, showing off her Wilder dimples to perfection. "My friends are going to be so jealous! You have a Harley."

He threw his head back and laughed. *Leave it to his daughter to be impressed with the motorcycle.* "Do I need to buy you a leather jacket, too?

Her eyes widened and she nodded.

"Hey, you two. Can I come up?" Jamie called from the bottom of the ladder.

"Yeah, Mom, come on up."

Wyatt saw her head pop up through the hole in the floor a moment later. Her eyes went round when they rested on him and Samantha sitting on the hay bale.

"Are you okay, baby?"

"I'm fine, Mom. It's just kind of a shock, but I guess I should have guessed."

"Why?" he asked.

"Because your eyes are the same color as mine and mom told me I had my dad's eyes."

"That you do, pumpkin. They are kind of a trademark with my family."

"Do they still live here? I mean, do I have other grandparents that I don't know?"

"My parents don't live here in Laramie, but they aren't that far away. And yes, you have grandparents and some other aunts and uncles as well as cousins."

"Cool! I want to meet them."

He chuckled softly. "I'm sure you will—in time."

Jamie took the hay bale across from them. "I'm sorry, Sam. I never should have kept Wyatt's existence from you, and when he came back, I should have made sure you knew who he is."

"You never wanted to talk about him, Mom."

Jamie closed her eyes and rubbed her forehead as Wyatt frowned at her movements. "I know, baby. That time was difficult at best. Being seventeen and pregnant wasn't a good thing."

"You okay, Jamie?"

"Yeah, I just have a headache. The stress, I guess." Her gaze returned to Samantha. "We'll make it up to you, sweetie—both of us. Right, Wyatt?"

"Yes," he answered, shifting his attention to Sam.

"Actually we had planned on telling you tonight, Samantha. That's why we were going to Wyatt's for dinner later. Unfortunately, your Uncle's big mouth ruined it."

"We could still go over there Mom—maybe do something as a family?"

"You have to understand one thing Sam, your mom and I aren't together as a couple anymore."

"I know, but that doesn't mean we can do things as a family, does it?"

His worried gaze met Jamie's across the loft, before it returned to his daughter. He knew for certain Samantha wanted them back together again so they could be a family and he wouldn't mind it either, but he didn't think that's what Jamie wanted. "We'll just take things slow, okay? I'll spend as much time with you as I can, but I do have to work and sometimes my schedule is messed up."

Samantha's shoulder lifted in a half shrug. "It's okay. I know you have to work and Mom is going to school. That's why we live with grandma and grandpa right now. Right, Mom?"

I didn't know she was going to school.

"Yeah. We'll be getting our own place soon." Jamie stood and wobbled a little on her feet and her face crinkled in pain.

"Are you sure you're okay? You look pale."

"I'm fine. It's just a little dizziness from standing up too fast." She looked at Samantha and said, "We should get back in the house, baby. Your uncle and aunt are worried about you."

"Okay, Mom."

"I'll go down first." He grasped the top of the ladder and moved a couple of rungs down. "Be careful. This ladder probably needs to be repaired. It's a little wobbly."

Once his feet touched the floor, Samantha came down right behind him and Jamie behind her. The ripe round ass cheeks that met his eyes when Jamie came down the ladder almost had him coming in his jeans and he groaned silently.

Damn! She's got the prettiest ass in the whole county!

He cleared his throat nervously when her eyes met his as her feet touched the floor and she frowned.

They all moved toward the house as the early afternoon sun reflected off the sliding glass doors. Stepping up on the back deck, Samantha broke the silence between him and Jamie with her bubbly chatter until they were almost to the rear of the structure.

Jamie stopped just as she reached the deck and grasped the handrail. Her knuckles turned white from the death grip she held on the wood. He moved back toward her and murmured, "Jamie?" Sweat dotted her forehead and her face had a pasty white color to it. When he grasped her hand, it was cold to the touch. "Jamie? Are you okay?"

"No—I don't feel well," she whispered, right before her eyes rolled back in her head and she slid toward the floor.

He scooped her up in his arms before she made it to the ground beneath their feet. Moving toward the door, he vaguely heard Samantha asking what happened while he whispered her Jamie's ear, "Jamie—baby. Talk to me." Quickly giving Samantha instructions to open the doors, he moved inside and headed for the couch in the living room. The rest of her family gathered and followed him, their rapid fire questions echoing in his ears when he gently laid her down.

"Someone grab a cool washcloth," he instructed while he began checking her over, taking her pulse and scanning her body with his eyes. "Abby? Can you go out to my bike and grab my bag off the back? My stethoscope and stuff is in there."

"Sure," she answered as Chase came back from the kitchen with the washcloth.

"What's wrong with her, Wyatt?" Bonnie asked from near Jamie's feet.

"I don't know, Mrs. Wilder." His gaze met Jamie's mothers and the worried look in her eyes echoed the feelings going through him. Terror tried to grip his heart in an unyielding grasp, but he shook it off for Jamie's sake.

Abby returned a moment later with his bag and he set about trying to find out why Jamie had passed out. He checked her over as his mind and his heart did battle within. He systematically went over her from head to toe, checking her pupils, listening to her heart and lungs and whispered a silent 'thank you' when he heard the steady beat pounding in his ears.

Several moments later, she finally moaned and began to stir. Her eyes flittered open and her unguarded emotions shone bright as she skimmed his face for a moment.

"Wyatt?"

"Yeah, baby."

"What happened?"

"You passed out."

The emotions were masked again when she said, "That's crazy. I never pass out."

"Well, you did."

"And Dad carried you in the house, Mom," Samantha interjected.

"He did?" She looked straight at him and his heart flip-flopped in his chest. "You did?"

"Yeah."

Confusion rippled across her face. "Thanks."

"He checked you over too, Jamie," Bonnie said, drawing Jamie's gaze to her mother before it came back to him.

"So, what's the diagnosis, doc?" Jamie asked.

"I have no idea, but you need to see your family doctor and have some tests run—blood tests, maybe a CAT scan."

She sat up quickly, forcing him to move back. "That's ridiculous. I'm fine."

"Jamie, you aren't fine if you passed out. It's not normal."

"I...I just got lightheaded, that's all. It was probably the heat."

"It's not that hot out there." He skimmed over her still pale face. "You need to be examined."

"Didn't you just do that?"

"Not as thoroughly as I would have liked." Heat crawled up from his neck and splashed across his cheeks when he realized what his words sounded like. "What I meant was...

"We know what you meant, Wyatt," Chase growled from behind him.

"Chase!" Abby reprimanded. "Even if you don't like him, you can at least be civil."

"Believe me, sweetheart—I am being civil."

"Just knock it off, Chase. Even if you don't like it, he will be connected to this family for the rest of our lives," Jamie said.

"Not if I have anything to say about it," Chase countered.

"Well, you don't. He is Samantha's father whether you like it or not and he has a right to take up that role if he so chooses."

"He gave up that right when he skipped town," Chase added.

"That isn't for you to decide. I make that choice and so does Samantha." Jamie stood up suddenly and moaned softly as her hand went to her head.

"You need to sit down." Wyatt grasped her hand, forcing her to sit back down on the couch.

"Just stop, Wyatt. I have a migraine or something, that's all." She pulled her hand out of his and stiffened. "What do you care anyway?"

"I care more than you know," he whispered before he said louder, "Are you prone to migraines?"

"No."

"Then why do you think it's a migraine?"

"I've heard about the symptoms. The blurred vision, light sensitivity—I'm sure you know them as well, if not better than I do."

"Those describe several different kinds of problems, not just migraines. Is your vision blurred?"

Damn it! Why is she being so stubborn?

"A little," she murmured and rubbed her temples.

"Where does your head hurt?"

"Right behind my left eye."

He took his thumbs and pressed right under both of her eyes. "Does this hurt?"

"Mmm…a little."

"How much is a little?"

"Just a little…come on, Wyatt. This is crazy. I'm fine." She took a deep breath and stood.

With a glance at Bonnie and Charles, he pleaded, "Please make sure she sees a doctor. She probably needs at least a CAT scan, but she's obviously not going to listen to me. Damn stubborn woman."

Jamie stuck her tongue out at him.

"Oh, real mature, Jamie."

She rolled her eyes before she said, "I'm going to go upstairs and lie down for awhile."

Samantha stopped her as she reached the stairs. "Mom, are we still going to Dad's tonight for dinner?"

Jamie looked at him before her gaze moved back to Samantha. "I don't think we should."

"Your mom really isn't feeling up to it, Sam," Wyatt agreed.

"Why don't I just go then? I could spend some time with him since we really haven't gotten a chance to. Please Mom?"

He shrugged when she shot him a look. "She's welcome if it's all right with you."

Jamie rubbed her forehead again before she sighed heavily and said, "I suppose it would be all right. Just make sure she's home before it gets too late."

Samantha exclaimed, "Yes!"

"What time do you want her back here?" he asked as Jamie took a couple of steps up the stairs.

"Probably no later than ten."

"Not a problem."

"Be careful. She's everything to me," Jamie murmured when their eyes met over their daughter's head.

"Me too, Jamie."

She nodded and moved up the stairs, disappearing from sight a moment later, never aware that his gaze followed her until he couldn't see her anymore.

When his attention moved to Samantha, he said, "You need a jacket of some kind, Sam. It's cool on the bike even if it's warm right now."

"I'll be right back." She raced up the stairs while his attention returned to Chase and Abby.

"I think we need to talk, Chase, but not right now—not when Sam can hear."

"I don't care to hear anymore from you, Wyatt, even if Jamie explained how things went down. I have to put up with you because of Jamie and Samantha, but I don't have to like it."

Abby stepped up beside her husband and held out her hand. "I know we haven't met. I'm Abigail Wilder, but my friends call me Abby. It's nice to finally meet you."

He grasped her hand in a firm shake and Chase scowled. "Nice to meet you, Abby."

Her eyes narrowed slightly as she looked at his hand and returned to his face.

"How long have you and Chase been together?"

"A couple of years."

"You aren't from here either, though. New York?"

She smiled. "How did you guess?"

"Your accent. I spent some time in New York a few years ago."

Chase scowled. "When you should have been here?"

"All right, Chase. Fine. Let's go out back and get this over with because this hatred you feel toward me is just going to fester into a problem if we don't get it out in the open."

"After you buddy," Chase said as he indicated toward the back door with his head.

Wyatt sighed and asked, "Abby, can you keep Sam in here, please?"

"Sure."

"Thanks." Wyatt walked briskly toward the back of the house leading onto the deck. He no more than got outside and turned around before Chase swung and hit him square in the jaw. He flew back several feet and landed on the deck with a thud.

Chapter Seven

Wyatt grasped his chin in his hand and moved it around to make sure it wasn't broken before he said, "Do you feel better now?"

"Hell no! I'm just getting started," Chase growled.

"Well, I'm not going to let you hit me again. You got a freebee that time. Now, I suggest you sit down so we can talk this out."

Air rushed from between his lips as Chase took a seat in one of the patio chairs sitting near the table and Wyatt took the other one.

"I take it Jamie didn't tell you how things went down when I left."

"Not until a few days ago."

Wyatt shook his head and said, "I didn't want to leave. I told her I would quit school and we could raise the baby together—she wouldn't let me."

"She told me that much, but what I don't understand is why you let her drive you away."

"I was scared." He raked his hand through his hair. "God, I was so scared." He sighed heavily. "My girlfriend had just told me she would be having my child and I could see my whole career going down the toilet. Plus, I knew you, Justin, and Cole would kill me when you found out. None of you even knew we were having sex. Maybe I took the easy way out and let her make the decisions for the both of us, but I didn't know what else to do. How in the hell could I raise a baby? I worked a dead-end job that hardly paid enough to support my apartment and enough to eat for me, let alone a wife and child."

"Wife?"

"I would have married her."

"Did you tell her that?"

Wyatt shifted his eyes away for a moment before they returned to Chase. "Not in so many words I guess, but I told her I loved her and I knew she loved me, too. She said she didn't and walked out. You know I tried to get her to talk to me for several weeks before I finally gave up and left."

"Why didn't you contact her or Samantha in the last nine years then, Wyatt?"

"For the same reason, I guess. I knew when I finished my residency; I would be coming back here to practice. I took the chicken-shit way out, I know that. I can't take back what happened over the last nine years, but I can be a father to Samantha now, and I want to. I'll support Jamie and Samantha any way she will allow me too."

"Do you still love Jamie?"

Wyatt stood up and moved to the railing on the deck and looked out over the pasture behind the house. After several moments, he turned around. "I'm not sure. I care for her. I always will, but love her…" He shrugged. "We are so different now."

"Not so different you aren't attracted to her."

"I'll give you that. Yes, she can still wrap my dick in her hand and lead me around with it if she so chose."

"Watch it. This is my sister we're talking about."

"I'm giving you the facts. Yes, I'm still attracted to her. She doesn't have to do anything but breathe to get me wound up tighter than a spring. What's going to happen—I don't have a clue, but I'm here to stay, one way or the other."

"I'm glad to hear that, and I just might be able to keep Cole and Justin from killing you."

Wyatt chuckled. "I would appreciate it. I kind of like being alive."

"Your ability to continue to live in this town depends on how you treat Samantha and Jamie." Chase's eyes narrowed, pinning Wyatt where he stood. "See that you watch your step."

"Got it." Wyatt moved toward the back with Chase on his heels. Samantha and Abby both looked terrified when they reached the living room.

"You okay, Dad?"

"Yeah, pumpkin. I'm fine." He wrapped an arm around her shoulders. "You ready to go?"

With a quick, enthusiastic nod, she slipped on her coat and he followed her out the front without another word to Jamie's family.

* * * *

The hamburgers sizzled and the gas fire popped as the grease dripped from the meat. The giggles and screams of several preteen girls echoed through his backyard and he smiled when Samantha jumped into the crystal blue water of his pool. The surprise of finding out he was her father had faded in the last six weeks. She embraced the fact to the point she already had his heart wrapped tightly around her little finger and he would do anything for her.

She managed to convince him to let her have a swim party and barbeque at his house for her friends. "Just to introduce you to them as my dad," she'd said. He smiled and shook his head when she waved before she dove head first back into the pool.

The smile turned to a frown when his eyes fixed on the beautiful brown-haired woman who lounged in the sun off to his left. Jamie. She had insisted on being there with Samantha this afternoon, and her presence did nothing for his libido. He hadn't touched her since the day she had passed out and now his palms itched with the need to run his fingers through her hair. She hadn't been to see a physician since that day and it made him mad to no end. Something wasn't right with her off-again on-again headaches, but he couldn't convince her of that. Inhaling a deep breath and let it out with a rush of air, he closed the lid on the grill and headed in her direction.

"Can I get you something to drink? The food is almost ready," he asked when he reached her side.

Her face turned up to him and his gut clenched with need when she flashed him her delicious dimples. "No, thanks. I'm good."

You certainly are.

With a quick shake of his head, he tried to clear the images of her beneath him from his mind. "Would you care to help me get the rest of the stuff set up so the girls can eat? The burgers are pretty much done, but I need to get the ketchup and stuff from the kitchen. Four hands are better than two."

"Sure," she said and stood beside him, the scent of coconut oil and Jamie invading his senses.

Once they were inside, she asked, "Whatever made you decide to allow Sam to have this party over here, anyway? I mean, you've got a great backyard with the pool and everything, but come on."

"She's no different than her mother, you know. She's already figured out flashing those Wilder dimples at me will get her just about anything she wants." He pulled open the refrigerator and grabbed several bottles of condiments.

The next thing he knew, the heat from Jamie's body warmed his back as she slipped her arms around him.

"Just about anything?" she murmured in his ear.

"Jamie," he whispered and closed his eyes.

Her lips grazed his shoulder as her warm breath brushed against his skin. His hand grasped the ketchup bottle so tight, he thought for sure it would crack under the pressure. The tips of her fingers skimmed the muscles of his abdomen and she chuckled behind him when he groaned softly.

Little witch.

"Dad?" Samantha called, poking her head inside the house.

Jamie stepped back and he turned around to find Sam at the sliding door, water dripping to the ground around her feet.

"Yeah?" He cleared his throat before he tried again when the first answer came out in a half squeak. "Yeah?"

"I think the burgers are done."

His gaze caught Jamie's and he knew the fire she ignited in him also burned brightly inside of her. Her brown eyes sparkled in the afternoon sun streaming through the window. "I'll be right there."

The glass opening slid shut with a soft whoosh.

Jamie flipped her hair off her shoulder as a teasing grin rippled across her lips. She cocked her perfectly arched eyebrow while her eyes skimmed down his chest and centered a moment on his cock, which was straining against the front of his jeans, before they returned to his face.

Damn it!

He cleared his throat. "Grab that plate with the lettuce and stuff on it and I'll take the other things." Once he stepped around her, he sighed heavily, trying to get the raging desire racing through his veins under control.

Once they reached the warm sunshine, the giggles and chatter of the girls around them dissipated the tension he felt. He pulled the hamburgers off the grill and set them on the table. A smile lifted his lips as the group dove for the hamburgers and other food before they moved off to find somewhere to sit.

He fixed himself a plate and took a seat at the table across from Jamie. "I bought a cake, too. I figured since her birthday was next week, we could celebrate it today. That is, if you don't mind."

Jamie's shoulders lifted in a shrug of nonchalance, but frown lines appeared between her eyebrows. "I hadn't really thought much about it yet. She and I usually go to the mall or something for her birthday. I've never really thrown her a birthday party."

"We can count this as one, then."

Her frown deepened and she avoided looking at him.

"What's wrong?"

"Nothing."

"Bullshit, Jamie. I know you well enough to know when something is bothering you."

She met his stare across the table. "That's just it, you don't know me at all anymore."

"That didn't stop you from coming on to me in the kitchen."

Jamie looked over her shoulder to make sure the girls were far enough away; they couldn't hear her. She leaned toward him and said, "I'm horny, Wyatt. It's been a while." A teasing smile lifted the corners of her mouth and his heart slammed against his ribs. "At least a few weeks."

He knew damned well what she meant as he remembered the tryst a couple of weeks previously. It was obvious she changed the subject to avoid telling him what bugged her. "Quit trying to sidetrack me. What's bothering you?"

She shrugged again and looked at the food in her hand. "I haven't had the money to be able to have a big party for her or buy her something really nice for her birthday." Air rushed from between her lips in a heavy sigh. "I refused to take anything extra from my parents."

"I'm not trying to outdo you. I have a lot of years to make up for when I wasn't even around for her birthday."

"I realize that, but you are making it look like I've been slack in taking care of her, even if you aren't trying to. You have the money now to do what you want to for her and I don't—not yet, anyway. Once I get my license, I'll be able to get our own place and support her like I should." She popped a potato chip into her mouth and then frowned.

"That reminds me. You never did tell me what you were studying."

Her pink tongue appeared and swiped the ketchup from the edge of her mouth. He stifled the groan that rumbled in his chest.

"I'll have my registered nurse's license in a few months. I just graduated from the program. I'm studying for my test right now, but its slow going."

He cocked an eyebrow and asked, "Nursing license?"

"Don't look so surprised. I've always wanted to be a nurse."

"I didn't know that."

"It just goes to show you how much you didn't know about me."

"When do you take your test?"

"In a few weeks." She took a bite of her hamburger and he wasn't sure if he had ever seen anything so erotic in his life, when images of those lips wrapped around his cock zipped across his mind.

"Do you need help studying?"

Why the fuck did I volunteer for that? The last thing I need is to be in close contact with her.

When she smiled, his heart flipped in his chest. "I can always use some extra help. You would probably be pretty good at it since you know the medical side of things already."

"I can try, anyway. I'm not perfect, but I remember the hell I went through studying for my medical boards."

"Okay—sure."

"How about if you come back over here later tonight? You can take Samantha home and bring your book back. I'm not working tomorrow so I don't have to worry about getting up early in the morning. I'll even get some refreshments and we can have an all-nighter if you want." The dimples appeared and he realized what he said.

Shit! Wrong phrase.

"What I meant…"

"Mmm…it's been awhile for one of those, too."

He bit the inside of his mouth to keep from commenting. He really didn't want to know how long it had been for her when he knew exactly how long it had been for him. Way too long. His pants tightened around his cock again and he shifted on the bench.

Deciding to change the subject, he asked, "So, anymore episodes of passing out?"

The frown appeared again. "Not really."

"Jamie?"

"All right, yes. It happened again the other day while I cleaned out one of the horse's stalls in the barn."

"You have got to see a doctor. This could be really serious, baby. I'm worried about you."

She cocked an eyebrow and he realized the sweet nothing that had slipped from his mouth without thought. It had always been his endearment for her, but he hadn't called her that in quite a while—not since the night she had passed out and he had carried her into the house.

"You don't need to worry."

"Why not? If nothing else, you are the mother of my child. I have a right to worry."

"No, you don't." She stood and headed for the house with her plate in hand.

With a heavy sigh, he picked up his own and followed. Once they reached the kitchen and placed their plates in the sink, he took her by the arm and swung her around to face him. "Tell me why I don't have a right to worry about you. It's not like we can just pretend our relationship nine years ago never happened."

Yanking her arm out of his grasp, she spat, "Maybe I wish it never had."

"Is that really true?"

Turning her back to him and placing her hands on the counter, she sighed and bent her head. "I don't know, Wyatt. I sometimes wonder what my life would have been like if we had never met that day at the pizza parlor." She lifted her head and turned toward him. When their eyes met, he could see the pain in her gaze. "Don't you ever wonder?"

"No."

"Why not?"

"Because I wouldn't have had the best nine months of my life. I wouldn't have a beautiful daughter who I adore and I wouldn't have been with the most gorgeous woman in Laramie." He skimmed his fingers across her jaw. "I wouldn't trade those things for anything in the world."

Her lips parted in silent invitation as he focused on her mouth. Stepping closer, her breasts brushed against his bare chest and her nipples puckered under her t-shirt, almost making him groan out loud. He bent his head, hell-bent on feeling her lips under his. When their mouths were close enough, he could feel her warm breath against his lips, he heard the sliding glass door open with a soft whoosh.

He groaned softly and stepped back.

"Dad?"

"Yeah, Sam."

"Can we go back in the pool?"

"Sure. We'll be back out there in a second. Wait until we're out there to watch you and your friends, though."

"Okay. Hurry up, then."

He chuckled and shook his head. "Impatient, isn't she?"

Jamie smiled and said, "Yep. Just like her mother."

His thumb skimmed over her lower lip and her tongue darted out to touch his skin. "You weren't impatient before. Seems to me, if I remember correctly, you were pretty patient with me." Desire zinged from the finger she drew into her mouth straight to his shaft.

Releasing his thumb, she murmured, "Mmm…if you mean me waiting for you to call me after I slipped you my number, then yes, I guess I was pretty patient. You took an awfully long time to call."

"I couldn't get over the shock of it."

Surprise registered across her face and her eyes widened. "Shock?"

"The prettiest girl in the whole place had just given me her number. How else can I explain it?"

She stepped away and pulled open the refrigerator. "Oh pllleeaase! The prettiest girl, my butt."

"That's pretty nice, too."

Glancing over her shoulder, she rolled her eyes and shut the fridge. "Whatever. I'm sure you had your share of women in California. With those blue eyes and nice body…"

He smiled. "Nice body?"

"You had your share of girls chasing you back then, Wyatt, so don't act like you don't know. I'm sure there are at least a few still chasing."

His shoulders lifted in a shrug when he leaned against the counter behind him. "I haven't been celibate, if that's what you mean."

Her mouth turned down in a frown. "I didn't think you would have been. I know I haven't been either." She brought the can of soda to her lips as she shot him a glance over the rim.

The thought of her with someone else sent an ache through his chest, he didn't like.

"Are you coming? We want to go back into the pool," Samantha called.

"All right, Sam." He tilted his head toward the door and asked Jamie, "Shall we?"

"After you."

They settled in two lounge chairs once they reached the concrete that surrounded the pool. He kept the conversation light as they watched the girls laughing and playing for the next couple of hours.

When the sun began to set, he went inside the house and brought out the cake he had bought for Samantha's birthday, complete with ten candles. The glow lit up the small space around the pool and sparkled on the lashes of his little girl when she flashed him the biggest smile he had ever seen. She rushed around the table and threw her arms around his waist and hugged him tight. "Thanks, Dad."

"You're welcome, pumpkin," he said, a little choked up himself with tears as he hugged her back.

After his conversation with Jamie earlier, he had decided to hold off on Samantha's gift until he could get her alone. He didn't want Jamie to feel bad and he knew once she saw the diamond necklace he had purchased, she would be pissed. They had a small truce at the moment and he didn't want to ruin that—not right now.

Once the cake and ice cream had been devoured, the other girls went home and he walked Jamie and Samantha to her truck.

Samantha hugged him again and he kissed her on the cheek. "I hope you enjoyed your party."

"It was awesome."

"Good. Now, get in the truck so your mother can get you home." After Samantha ran around to the passenger side and got in, he opened the door for Jamie and she slid inside the cab and he shut it behind her.

She unrolled the window and said, "I'll be back in about an hour. Let me get her settled and all."

"Sure."

"You're coming back, Mom?"

"Yeah. Wyatt is going to help me study."

"I'm just going to clean up some of the mess in there that the fifteen nine and ten year old girls made."

"Oh, Dad!" Samantha rolled her eyes and he laughed.

"I'll see you in a little bit then. Be careful."

"I will. See you in a few." She smiled and his heart stopped in his chest. Rolling up the window, he stepped back and watched her put the truck in reverse before she backed out of the driveway.

When she finally disappeared around the corner of his street, he ambled back inside and started to gather the miscellaneous cups and plates scattered around the house and back yard.

Chapter Eight

The ring of the doorbell shocked Wyatt out of his reverie. His thoughts had drifted to Jamie and their little tryst in the kitchen, making him hornier than he had been in at least six weeks. Now she had returned and he tried to calm the desire racing along his nerve endings.

She came back so I can help her study, not for me to take her to bed and make love to her like I want to.

The bell let out another tinkling ring and he headed toward the front to answer it.

The heavy wooden panel swept open when he pulled the handle and said, "You're quick."

She stepped inside and a smile lifted the corners of her mouth. "I didn't want to waste any time." Placing her backpack on the dining room table, she said. "I checked my appointment time when I got home and I have to take my test earlier than I thought. It's actually scheduled for next week."

"I guess we had better get busy, then." Moving into the kitchen, he asked, "What would you like to drink before we get started?"

"Uh…soda or whatever is fine. I know there is still some beer left, but since I need to drive home later, I had better not drink."

He nodded. "That's probably a good idea." Two sodas from the refrigerator and a bag of potato chips from the pantry were sat on the table before he pulled out a chair. "So, what do you want to focus on?"

She spread out her notes and study book in front of them. "Probably the medications would be a good start. I'm confused with all the different types and what they are for."

"What are you planning to specialize in?"

"What do you mean?"

"Like emergency medicine, cardiac, geriatrics…you know."

"Oh. I'm not sure, actually. I think the ER would be really interesting, fast-paced and all that."

He took a sip from the can in his hand before he leaned back in the chair. "It can be. Sometimes it's really boring and very tedious."

With a frowned, she grabbed the potato chips, pulling the bag open before she popped one into her mouth. "Why did you go into emergency medicine then?"

A groan rumbled in his chest when her tongue peeked out and slipped along her lips. "For the same reasons you mentioned. The adrenaline rush to some extent, but there are definitely downtimes."

One shoulder lifted in a half shrug. "True. It can't be all high gear."

His lips twitched into a small smile as he pictured her rushing around the emergency room to do his bidding and maybe a quick sneak off into one of the supply closets.

That could be interesting.

He shifted uncomfortably in the chair when his cock came to full attention and pressed insistently against the fly of his jeans.

* * * *

Jamie noticed the sparkle in his blue eyes and the smile on his kissable lips. "What are you smiling for?"

"Who, me?"

"Yes, you. I see that little smirk." She pointed at his mouth and cocked a questioning eyebrow.

"Nothing." His grin got bigger his perfect white teeth gleamed in the florescent light of the dining room.

Damn it! If I get any hornier, I'm going to jump him right here and make him fuck me on the dining room table.

"Yeah, right, Wyatt. I know you better than that."

"I just thought it would be interesting for us to work together at the emergency room—after you get your license, of course."

She narrowed her eyes and contemplated working with him on a daily basis. *Mmm…bad idea, probably.*

Bringing the subject back around to what she had come there for, she said, "We should get busy on this studying; otherwise we'll be here all night." She opened her book and his hand came across the table to pull it out of her hands.

"Doesn't bother me. I told you that earlier."

"Well, no sleep for this girl tends to make her really bitchy."

"Mmm…that I do remember."

She wanted to smack the smirk right off his face, remembering all too well the several times she got no sleep after spending the night with him. He would run her home at the wee early morning hours to sneak into the house before anyone else got up. Not an easy task when her brothers were early risers to work with the horses.

"Can we get busy?" *Shit! The smirk returned.* "On studying?"

"Oh—yeah—right." He opened the book and began firing questions at her like bullets zinging around the room. She had to stop him on several occasions to ask a question about something. With more patience than she contained herself, he would give her a lengthy explanation, telling her more than she would ever remember.

Two hours later he closed the book.

"What? I'm sure there are more in there you could ask me."

"You know this stuff. You'll do fine on your test."

She stood and walked to the window to peer out into the moonlit backyard. A moment later he moved behind her and placed his hands on her shoulders. Unable to stop herself, she leaned back against his chest, accepting his solid strength. She shivered when his hands moved down her arms.

"Do you still have your suit? We could go for a swim."

Goose bumps rose on her skin as she whispered, "It's a bit cool for a swim isn't it?"

"No, but if you'd rather, there is always the hot tub."

His thumbs kneaded the soft flesh of her shoulders, working the tense knots from her muscles and she moaned softly when her head rested fell back against his shoulder. "God, that feels heavenly. You always were good with your hands."

The soft caress of his lips near her ear had her pussy clenching tight while she struggled to relieve some of the pressure building between her thighs. "Why don't we get in the hot tub and I'll work those muscles," he paused his words for a moment as his warm breath flittered along her skin, before he continued, "Until they are nice and relaxed. You'll sleep like a baby tonight."

Closing her eyes as desire zipped along her nerve endings, she sighed and gave into the feelings he stirred. He always knew exactly what to do to get her wound up and begging for more, and sleep was the last thing on her mind at the moment. "Lucky for you, I left my suit on under my clothes."

He chuckled softly and shivers raced down her arms.

"Let me change and grab a couple of towels. If you want, I'll meet you out there."

When she nodded, he stepped back, taking his warmth with him. His reflection in the glass gave her the perfect view of his broad shoulders, slim waist and impossibly perfect ass when he moved toward the bedroom. Shaking her head, she slid open the glass door and stepped outside as the warmth of the evening air hit her face.

The light that illuminated the hot tub beaconed when she walked toward it. Once she reached the side, she unbuttoned her jeans and slipped them down over her hips, stepped out and laid them across a nearby chair. She lifted her t-shirt over her head and put it on top of her pants, just as she heard Wyatt behind her when he groaned softly. Smiling to herself, she sat on the side of the hot tub and swung her legs into the water.

The steamy water lapped at her legs and inched up when she sank down until it reached her shoulders. She tipped her head back on the side of the tub, but didn't open her eyes when Wyatt sank into the warmth next to her with a soft sigh.

"I love hot tubs," he whispered. "Turn around."

She cracked open one eye as she lifted her head and turned her back to him. Thighs cradled her ass, and she fought the urge to grind it against the bulge precariously close to her back. He draped her hair over her shoulder, before his thumbs found the tight muscles at her neck. Dropping her head toward her chest, she moaned softly as his supple hands worked the knots from her neck and shoulders.

"Good?"

"Mmm…fabulous."

"Why don't you tell me what you've been doing the last nine years? We haven't really had a chance to just talk."

"Very true." She rolled her head to one side. "After Sam was born, I stayed with my parents for a few years, but I worked at Johnson's Grocery in order to help with bills and stuff." She moaned, and said, "You have no idea how good that feels."

He chuckled again.

"Anyway. I finally moved out and got a place of my own that I could afford and my mom watched Sam while I worked. I did pretty well until the store laid me off because business went to shit when Wal-Mart came into town."

"Yeah. I can imagine. They tend to do that when they build a store."

"That's when I decided to move back in with my parents and get my nursing degree. It's been a long three years, but I'm done now and things will be a lot better with more money coming in."

"You know I'll help you with her."

She changed the subject. "So, where did you go after you left here?"

"Los Angeles."

"And?"

"It's not the same as here. Way too fast paced for me. I'm just a simple guy."

"Simply gorgeous," she murmured.

His hands wandered down her arms and he pulled her back against his chest. Warm lips whispered softly against the skin of her neck. Her nipples puckered against the top of her bikini and heat flooded between her thighs. Her pussy throbbed and filled at the contact of his mouth. Her body remembered his touch, every whisper of his fingers and every brush of his lips.

Her head fell back on his shoulder when he skimmed up her neck with his tongue. He nibbled her earlobe with his teeth, taking the soft flesh and biting softly. "Do you want me, baby?"

She almost whimpered but groaned instead. "God, yes!"

He turned her in his arms and settled her on his lap, her thighs spread wantonly around his waist. His mouth swooped down and took possession of her lips, groaning his own frustration into her mouth. Opening for him, she allowed his tongue to dance with her own while her hands wound around his shoulders and settled in the hair at the nape of his neck. Skimming his fingers up her side, he found her breast with his palm and kneaded the soft flesh.

His free hand slid under the hair at her neck and untied the knot holding her top together. The material slipped down, exposing her bare breasts. His mouth left her lips and wandered across her cheek. Lips brushed her jaw before he nibbled his way down her throat. She arched her back in offering as she felt his warm breath caress her chest on his search downward. She almost screamed when his lips settled over her nipple.

Whimpering softly when his teeth nipped at the hard nub, she almost slipped off his lap when he sucked, pulling it deep between his lips. His left hand rolled the other nipple between his fingers, sending electricity straight to her pussy. The hand finally abandoned her breast and slipped down her stomach, finding the waistband of her bottoms. A moment later, his thumb glanced across her clit, sending her desire spiraling out of control.

"Oh, God," she moaned, gyrating her hips to the rhythm his thumb set.

"I need to get these off," he murmured against her chest when his finger left her clit and she whimpered softly. He moved far enough away so she was able to drop her legs and he could slip her bottoms off.

Awareness returned slightly as she saw her bikini float away from them on the roll of the water from the jets of the hot tub. She knew she wasn't about to deny herself or him. A small smile lifted the corners of her mouth when their eyes met and she moved toward him, pushing him back against the side of the tub. "My turn," she whispered before her lips claimed his and her hands found the waist of his swim trunks. She slipped her palms inside and worked the elastic down his buttocks until they were loose enough and she could push them down around his feet. He kicked them off as her tongue delved into his mouth and her hand found his rock hard cock standing proudly against his abdomen.

A low growl left his throat when she caressed his length, sliding up and down as he rocked his hips in time to her stroke. Pulling his mouth away, he whispered, "You're torturing me, you know."

She smiled softly, and then slid her tongue along his bottom lip. "I know, but you love it."

His eyes rolled back as he groaned and laid his head against the side of the tub. "You know I do."

Her teeth nibbled at his neck where his heart beat frantically at the base of his throat. "I would wrap my lips around your cock, but kind of hard to do in here."

Peering between heavily laden eyes, he said, "I'm too wound up for that right now." He grabbed her ass cheeks, spreading her thighs and settling her pussy over his hard length so he could push inside.

She arched her back and moaned, "Oh, fuck."

Her pussy swallowed his entire length and when she clenched her vaginal muscles around him, she felt him swell inside her even further.

"Incredible, isn't it? It's always been this way between us, Jamie. No one else could ever do this for me."

He lifted her hips and dropped her back against his groin when his hips surged toward her. The water slapped at the sides of the tub. Their mingled cries of satisfaction echoed in the deserted backyard and she realized how loud they were getting as their mutual climax raced to the surface. She slanted her mouth across his when the tingling awareness of her orgasm start in her toes and race up her legs to explode in her belly, sending stars bursting behind her eyelids. His hips surged against her, slamming into her groin when his own end teetered on the edge. With a roar of satisfaction, he crushed her to his chest and growled in her ear.

She laid her head against his shoulder while their rapid breathing mingled and she tried to calm her racing heart. He was right. It had always been this way between them. He rocked her world when he made love to her and that hadn't changed.

When the desire had finally calmed, she pushed against his shoulders and he let her slide out of his embrace. Her bikini bottoms floated by them as his swim trunks followed not far behind and they laughed together at the sight.

Reaching over, she grabbed hers and pulled them beneath the surface of the water so she could slip them back on. She snagged his trunks and dangled them from her fingers in front of him with a saucy smile on her lips. He reached for them but she pushed away, taking his trunks with her, daring him to come after them with her eyes.

He cocked an eyebrow as his turquoise eyes twinkled. "Are you daring me?"

"Could be." She let the dimples peek out of her cheeks, knowing how much he loved them and taunted, "Come and get 'em, doc."

Without warning, he dove for her and she squealed, trying to roll out the side of the hot tub, forgetting completely that her top still dangled below her breasts. He grabbed her waist and pulled her back into the tub with him, but not before she threw his trunks several feet to the concrete with a wet plop. Startled, she met his gaze and swallowed hard when his lips turned up in a wicked-as-sin smile and he pulled her toward him. "Now, Wyatt..."

"Mmm...yes?" His lips nibbled the side of her neck.

"I'm only teasing," she murmured even though a moan bubbled in her throat.

"Teasing, huh?"

"Yeah, I'll go get them for you."

He reached behind her, untied the bottom string of her top and threw it out of the tub before she could even suck in a breath. "Okay. Go get them, then."

"Without my top?" she asked, pushing against his shoulders.

He lifted his head and a teasing smile rippled across his mouth. "Of course." The look on her face must have been hilarious because he chuckled softly. "What's the matter, Jamie—chicken?"

"I'm not chicken," she huffed, and stood up, swinging her legs over the side of the tub. Deciding to tease him a bit herself, she sauntered slowly to where their clothing lay in a wet heap on the concrete. She turned toward him, hooked the bottoms of her bikini with her thumbs and slowly peeled them down, inch by inch. His gaze got hotter and hotter. Once she reached her knees, she dropped them in a plop at her feet.

He growled low in his throat and leaped over the rim of the tub in one motion. Slowly stalking toward her, his hard cock bobbed against his stomach as he moved. With a squeak, she turned and dashed for the back door of the house. Managing to get it open before he reached her, she laughed out loud when he swept her up in his arms and stepped inside.

"Now, what are you gonna to do?" he asked, his purposeful strides moved toward his bedroom. Her lips grazed his throat and he moaned softly.

"Let you make love to me again," she murmured.

"I could do that all night."

"I'm up for an all-nighter. How about you?"

"You're a witch. I haven't been this damned horny in years."

She chuckled softly against his skin. "Mmm..." Running her tongue up his throat, she said, "I'll take that as a compliment."

He walked into his bedroom and kicked the door shut behind them, before he let her slide down his body until her feet touched the floor. Framing her face with his hands, he softly kissed her lips and then slid his tongue along the bottom one, before delving into her mouth. Their tongues dueled for a moment, bringing her desire to scorching temperatures. He lifted his head and told her, "God, you taste incredible."

His hand found her bare breast and he let his palm rasp across the nipple until she arched toward his touch. "I love when you touch me."

He chuckled softly as his lips whispered along her chest and downward, taking her nipple in his mouth. She wound her hands in his hair and pressed his head harder against her while he laved at the nipple. One hand slipped down her stomach until he reached the nest of curls guarding her sex. She almost screamed when he avoided touching her clit, but instead moved his hand around to grasp her ass. Never moving his mouth from her breast, both hands grasped her butt cheeks and lifted her in his arms. She wrapped her legs around his waist and he moved toward the bed.

He laid her down softly across the sheets and finally met her gaze. "I want you so bad, I ache for you."

His lips whispered down her stomach, licking the skin of her abdomen, stopping momentarily to play with the dangling earring at her belly button. She quivered under his mouth when he moved slowly downward. Again, he avoided her aching center, kissing her thighs, her knees, her ankles and her feet before moving back up her legs.

"God, Wyatt, please."

"Please what, Jamie? Tell me what you want, baby."

"Eat me, fuck me, do something, please. You're driving me crazy."

His warm laughter ruffled the curls between her thighs right before his tongue touched her clit and she almost flew apart at the seams. He toggled it a few times before moving to her vagina and spearing it with his tongue. The pad of his thumb found the hardened nub as his tongue danced over her pussy lips, coaxing her to come for him.

He lifted his head and she could feel his soft words against her skin when he whispered, "Come for me, Jamie." She almost screamed, but instead moaned his name as her juices flooded from her center and he lapped at her pussy until she had nothing left.

Kissing the insides of her thighs, then her stomach before he reached her lips, she moaned when he slipped his tongue inside her mouth as his cock nudged at her aching core. They moaned together when he slipped into her pussy, clear to the root of his cock, and she wrapped her legs around his hips.

He lifted his head and his lips grazed her cheek until he nudged against her ear with his nose. "So warm, so tight. You feel incredible. I'll never get enough of you."

She locked her heels behind him, urging him on with pressure against his buttocks. "Fuck me, Wyatt. Hard and fast. I don't want easy from you."

"I won't last long that way, baby."

"I don't care. We have all night for slow and easy." She urged him on by lifting her hips.

He lifted his chest and pulled her legs up so they rested across his forearms. His hips rocked, slamming into hers with such force she had to put her hands on the headboard to keep from sliding as she moaned, *"Yes. Yes. Yes."*

Her climax crashed over her like the waves cresting against the shore and she whispered his name on a sigh. He followed her shortly afterward as he growled in her ear and she felt his seed coat the inside of her vagina.

She stiffened in his arms when realization hit her.

Fuck! We didn't use a condom.

Chapter Nine

"Shit!" She squirmed before she said, "Wyatt, get off."

He lifted his head and looked into her eyes. "What's wrong?"

"We didn't use a condom. Not this time and not in the hot tub."

He pulled out of her with a soft groan and rolled onto his back beside her, draping his arm across his eyes. "Shit! God Jamie, I'm sorry. For what it's worth, I'm clean."

"I never doubted that, but I got pregnant with Samantha being on birth control with you."

He moved his arm and peered at her with one eye. "Aren't you on something now?"

"Yes. I hope it's enough. It wasn't last time between us."

Rolling onto his side, he propped himself on his elbow and grasped a piece of her hair between his fingers. "Well, it took more than once before. Hopefully, it didn't happen this time."

"God, I hope not."

He frowned.

"Don't get me wrong, I love our daughter with all of my heart and I'm glad you are her father, but I don't want another child. Not right now anyway, and that means not with you or anyone else."

The frown lines between his eyebrows deepened.

Air rushed from between her lips in a heavy sigh. "I'm fucking this all up." She sat up on the side of the bed, grabbed one of his t-shirts off the chair where he had thrown it sometime during the day and slipped it over her head. It would have to do until she could retrieve her own clothes. "I should go."

"Why?"

Glancing in his direction, she bit her lip and frowned. *Bad idea.* Her gaze wandered down his chest, across his six-pack abs and came to rest on his semi-soft cock before ricocheting back to his eyes. *Good grief, the man could put the men in Playgirl to shame.*

He reached over and ran his finger down her arm, sending goose bumps skittering across her flesh. "I thought you were going to stay all night."

"Well I…"

"We could take a shower. I've dreamt of making love to you in there since I saw you again at the hospital."

Closing her eyes, she and tried to get her rioting emotions and libido under control. She didn't know he moved until she felt his lips.

"Stay with me, Jamie." His tongue traced the shell of her ear. "I want to wake up with you next to me in the morning."

She wanted to—God only knew how much she wanted to. Her feelings for him hadn't changed in nine years and having him here again, played havoc with her emotions. She'd tried convincing herself, her friends, even him, that she didn't love him—had never loved him, but it was a huge lie. Falling in love with him nine years ago had been the easiest thing she'd ever done, but allowing her heart to love him now would be the hardest thing she could think of. Each time he came near her and every time he touched her, she wanted to melt into his arms and plead for him to keep her safe, take care of her and love her again, like he used to.

"Please? Let me fall asleep with you in my arms," he whispered and she knew she couldn't tell him no, especially when she wanted it as much as he did.

"Okay, but I have to go first thing in the morning."

He stood and pulled the sheet back on the bed before he grabbed the edge of the shirt she wore and slipped it over her head. "I want your skin next to mine," he said, wadding up the shirt and tossed it back across the chair. "Come here."

She moved back next to him and he wrapped his arm around her as he pulled her to his side. Tossing the sheet over them, she snuggled against him and laid her head on his chest. Soft curls tickled her cheek. Her fingers slid through the hair and she heard a low groan rumble beneath her face. He grasped her fingers and intertwined them with his own.

The moonlight filtered through the curtains, slanting a silver path across their bodies when she tossed her leg over his thigh and fitted her body to the curve of his.

We always did seem to fit perfectly together.

His lips grazed her forehead softly and his free hand skimmed along her shoulder in a feathery caress.

Does he love me? I wish I knew.

Her heart settled peacefully into a slow rhythm and his breathing calmed and became regular. She knew he slept when his soft snores reached her ears and she smiled wistfully. It had been a long time since she'd spent the night with a man, any man, much less Wyatt Crossland.

She looked at their fingers still entwined and resting on his chest as thoughts began to race across her mind.

Could we possibly build a life together after all these years? We are still obviously attracted to each other, but could he love me again? Is it possible?

Sighing heavily, she pushed the 'what if's' out of her mind as she snuggled next to him and closed her eyes.

* * * *

Bright sunlight touched Wyatt's face as he groaned softly and rolled over. His hand touched soft womanly skin and he inhaled the sweet scent of the hair of the woman next to him. Jamie.

It wasn't a dream after all.

He smiled and opened his eyes slightly, only to see the curve of her waist and the nicest ass he had ever been privy to, snuggled up to his groin. He stifled a groan when she moaned in her sleep and pushed her bottom further against him. The brain between his legs obviously had a mind of its own this morning as it started to throb and ache with want for the sweet heat so enticingly calling his name.

"Are you just going to ignore me or what?"

Grazing the skin near his mouth, he chuckled softly. He should have known she was awake. "Mmm…nope," he murmured before he ran his tongue over the top of her shoulder. "But I thought you had to leave first thing this morning?"

She rolled over onto her back and her brown eyes sparkled with mischief in the early morning light. "I won't be missed at home. At least not for a little bit yet." One fingernail cut a path down his chest, following the line of hair across his stomach until she reached his cock, standing proudly and fully aroused. She peeked up through her lashes when she slid one finger across the head of his penis, spreading the drop of pre-cum that had gathered on the tip. He slowly closed his eyes when she spread the dew down his rock hard shaft until she reached the base and wrapped her hand around him.

Groaning low in his throat, he rocked his hips toward her when she slid her hand back up. "You just love to torture me, don't you?"

"Who me?" Her throaty chuckle met his ear. "I'm only returning the favor."

"I don't torture you." He sighed when she continued to stroke his cock with her hand—up and down, dragging whimpers from between his lips.

"Oh, yes you do. Every time I'm around you. All I want to do is drag you off to the bedroom." She shifted so they were chest to breast and she could slip her thigh between his. Her tongue whispered along his bottom lip, before she continued, "And demand you make love to me."

He opened his eyes and peered into hers while he tried to read the feelings behind the words. "Jamie I…" his voice trailed off when she kissed his chest. Her lips closed around his nipple and she bit softly, tearing an agonized groan from deep within him. Her hand continued to stroke his cock and her tongue laved at his nipple, severing all coherent thought from his mind. Lips moved south, following the line of hair down his abdomen with her tongue until her warm breath flittered across his straining cock. His hips lifted in time to the stroke of her hand until he felt the softness of her lips close over the head of his penis.

"Oh, God. Oh, God," he panted when her mouth engulfed him.

"Mmm," vibrated against him, shooting electricity clear to his balls, tightening them almost painfully against his body.

"Jamie, baby," he moaned, hoping she would heed the warning in his voice as he fought for control. "Baby, please." She released him from her mouth with a pop when she turned and peered up at him, a wickedly delicious smile gracing her lips. "As much as I love how that feels, I want inside you when I come."

She sat up and the next thing he knew, she straddled his hips, grinding her hot pussy against his groin, but not letting him slide inside her. "Condom?"

"Drawer," he groaned, reaching up beside the bed and pulled open the small nightstand. He retrieved the foil package, but she took it from his fingers, tore it open with her teeth and proceeded to roll the slippery latex over his full length.

"Damn, that's hot," she whispered when she skimmed her fingers back up to the tip once the condom was in place. She scooted up, held his penis in her hand and sank down until his cock was completely inside her hot pussy.

"God, I love the way you feel wrapped around me," he whispered as he watched her toss her hair behind her and arch her back. His hands grasped her breasts and rolled each nipple simultaneously while she moaned and rocked her hips.

Leaning forward, she placed her hands on his chest until he almost slid completely from her warmth, before she rocked back and re-sheathed him inside her heat. Her hair surrounded them like a cloud when she kissed his lips and traced his mouth with her tongue, before delving inside to duel with his.

"You—are—absolutely—incredible." His broken words brought a smile to her lips. He closed his eyes and whimpered softly. The heat built in his groan to a raging inferno as his balls felt like they were about to split wide open. "God, Jamie, please."

She rocked faster, grinding her pelvis against his while her own breaths came out in rasping pants and lusty moans until her cry of climax echoed off the walls. His own release followed shortly afterwards as he slammed into her heat, filling the condom to almost bursting proportions. Collapsing across his chest, her hair spread softly against him while they tried to bring their breathing back to a normal tempo.

After several minutes she lifted up and propped herself on his chest with her elbow. "As much as I would love nothing more than to stay here like this all day, I have to go." She lifted her hips, successfully unsheathing him from her warmth. When she rolled off the bed, she grabbed the t-shirt she'd worn briefly and headed for the bathroom.

He rolled on his side and watched her until she shut the door. Reaching down, he removed the condom and dropped it in the wastebasket at the side of the bed.

Damn, she's gorgeous.

A silly-ass, stupid grin was plastered all over his face when he thought of the night they'd shared.

Lying on his back, he folded his arms behind his head and stared at the ceiling while he played their night over in his mind. She had been as responsive as ever, meeting him thrust for thrust, lick for lick and everything in between. If nothing else, she had gotten better over time, if that was possible. When they were together before, their lovemaking had been good—better than good, but now, he could describe it as explosive.

He turned his head when she opened the door. She stood silhouetted against the bathroom light, her hair wildly tangled around her head. His fingers itched to comb through her curls and bring her lips to his, but he cleared his throat instead. "I think your jeans and shirt are in the living room."

"Actually, no, they're outside by the hot tub." Her eyes twinkled when she smiled. "Care to retrieve them for me?"

He cocked an eyebrow as he raked her from head to toe and back again. "And miss seeing your naked ass as you walk away? Mmm…not on your life, woman."

Huffing slightly, she sauntered toward him with the sexiest swing of her hips he'd ever seen. "Pretty please?" Her lip stuck out in a small pout when she stopped next to the bed and leaned over him. She ran her tongue over his bottom lip before she bit down slightly, and then soothed the sting with her tongue.

He growled low in his throat and then grabbed her around the waist, swinging her over him, depositing her flat on her back. Pinning her to the bed with his body, he said, "Depends on what's in it for me."

"Welll…" She ran her fingernail down his chest and he sucked in a ragged breath. "I might be persuaded to come back over here later."

"Might you, now."

"Uh-huh." The teasing glint in her eye had him wondering what she might be up to.

"Maybe for dinner? We could go out somewhere nice."

"Maybe."

He nibbled at the sides of her lips and she sighed when his tongue found the spot where her dimples usually creased her cheeks. He finally lifted his head and said, "Okay. I'll go get them." He rolled out on the opposite side, grabbed his jeans and slipped them on. He looked over his shoulder as she propped herself on her elbows and gave him as sexy-as-hell smile. He smiled in return and shook his head before he disappeared in search of her clothes.

The sun reflected off the sliding glass when he pulled it open. Her clothes still sat where she had left them the night before, draped across a chair near the hot tub. As he snatched them up in his hand, he turned to his left to find his neighbor peeking over the stone wall separating his house from hers.

"Good morning, Wyatt. Some party last night," Joan said with a quirk of her perfectly arched eyebrow.

He fought the urge to roll his eyes. "Morning, Joan."

"Where is your friend this morning?"

"I don't know who you're talking about."

Her gaze dropped to the obviously feminine blouse clutched in his hand. "Your female friend. If the noise I heard over here was any indicator, you sounded like you were having a good time." Her gaze raked his chest and he fought the urge to shiver in revulsion. He hadn't lived here long, but Joan had made it perfectly clear from the beginning she would keep him entertained, if he so chose, but he wasn't interested. Her collagen-filled lips, waxed eyebrows, obviously over-accentuated breasts and never without any makeup face, did nothing for him, even if he hadn't been with Jamie again. He preferred the woman he woke up with to have a pretty face without all the trappings—a good old country girl. She had to be comfortable in jeans and a t-shirt if the occasion warranted it, or a pretty dress if need be. He had the feeling Joan wouldn't be caught dead without her makeup.

"Oh, yeah, a good time was had by all, I assure you."

Her eyes narrowed and a frown pulled down the corners of her mouth. "You should have invited me. I'm sure I could help keep you satisfied, Wyatt. I get the impression one woman isn't enough for you."

"Trust me, Joan, this woman is plenty enough for me."

"Wyatt? What the hell is taking you so long?" Jamie asked when she peered outside. Her bare legs were obvious when one knee appeared through the opening. Joan's gaze ricocheted to where Jamie now stood and he didn't think her eyes could turn into slits with all the Botox in her face, but they did.

"Well, hello there," Joan said, and he could almost hear her grit her teeth. "I'm Joan, Wyatt's neighbor."

"Hello," Jamie replied, her wide eyed gaze zipping back to him.

"She's cute, Wyatt, but not what I would think would be your type, honey."

"Joan," he growled, but she didn't heed his warning.

"I mean, really. She's kind of flat chested in comparison. I know how much you like breasts and all. That blonde you had over here last week," she tapped her painted fingernail against her chin as she thought. "What was her name? Um...Janet, maybe? No." She snapped her fingers. "Amanda—that's it. Amanda. You sure had a good time with her in that hot tub of yours."

He could almost see the steam coming from Jamie's ears when she slid open the door the rest of the way and moved toward him. Not caring whether Joan knew she had no clothes on under his t-shirt, Jamie slipped out and grabbed her clothes from his hands before disappearing back inside the house.

Wyatt rounded on Joan and growled, "You bitch!"

"What?" Joan asked innocently.

"If you have screwed up my relationship with her, I will personally ruin you in this town. I'm sure your husband would be very interested to know where you spend your Saturday nights, especially when he's out of town."

She sucked in a frightened breath and her eyes widened. "How would you know?"

"I've seen the limo pull up outside. You really aren't very discreet, Joan, and I know Sebastian would love to hear about your trysts to the Kitty Club."

"You wouldn't dare."

Placing his hands on his hips, he said, "Wouldn't I? I have no qualms about making sure your circle of friends and your husband know about your *other* activities if you get in my way."

He couldn't see the iris of her eyes anymore when she glared at him and her lip curled into a snarl. "You'll be sorry you crossed me, Wyatt," she threatened before she disappeared back over her side of the wall.

Hurrying toward the back of the house, he called, "Jamie?" Calling her name again, he jumped when the next thing he heard was the front door slam. "Shit!"

Racing toward the entrance, he jerked it open just in time to hear her truck start. She jammed it into reverse and backed out of the driveway with a squeal of tires that bounced off the houses around his.

* * * *

Tears burned behind her eyes, threatening to fall at any moment as she jammed her feet into her jeans and pulled them up.

Fuck. Fuck. Fuck. Why the hell did I let him get to me?

She swiped at the moisture at the corner of her eyes, and then slipped her blouse on, quickly buttoning it.

I have to get out of here.

Dressing quickly, she walked toward the living room and grabbed her purse. Keys in hand, she disappeared out the front, slamming the wooden panel behind her in her frustration and headed for her truck. She ripped open the driver's side, slid inside and whipped it closed. Jamming the key into the ignition, she turned it and sighed when the engine growled to life just as she saw Wyatt appear, out of the corner of her eye. Her heart shattered in her chest when she took a moment to skim over his handsome face behind her tears, before she slipped the truck into reverse and backed out. The tires barked in protest when she hit the gas, leaving the only man she ever loved in the dust behind her.

She managed to reach her parent's house and disappear into her room before she let the tears fall in earnest. Burying her face in her pillow, she sobbed the gut-wrenching tears of a woman in love with a man who didn't love her in return.

He plays a good game. He almost convinced me that we might be able to fall in love again, but how could he love me if he was just with someone else last week? All I am is a piece of ass to him.

Her head whispered, "That's probably all you ever were. Did he really care about you even nine years ago?" Her heart demanded, "Of course he did. He said he loved you when you told him you were pregnant with Samantha. He would have quit school and raised her with you."

As her brain and her heart argued inside of her, she knew her body would react to his no matter whether he loved her or not. She wanted him like no other and that would never change. It hadn't in nine years, why would it now. He knew exactly what to do to make her body sing for his, cream for his and take him inside her, loving every minute he rocked her world as his cock stroked and fed the flames of her desire.

Her cell phone rang in her pocket and she rolled over before she pulled it free. Peering at the screen, her heart slammed against her ribs when she saw his name.

I'm not answering it. I don't want to talk to him right now.

She laid the phone on her nightstand and lay on her back to watch the sunlight bounce across the ceiling of her room.

A soft knock sounded to her left and she hesitated to answer. After a moment, she said, "Who is it?"

Samantha's face appeared and her worried expression made Jamie feel like shit. "Mom? Are you okay?"

"Yeah, baby. I'm fine. Come on in if you want to."

Sam came inside and the bed dipped from her slight weight when she sat down. "Where were you last night? You didn't come home."

Jamie scooted over and Samantha lay down beside her as she wrapped her arm around her daughter and Sam put her head on Jamie's shoulder.

She chewed her bottom lip, wondering if she should tell Samantha where she had actually spent the night. The last thing Sam need would be to get any ideas that her parents were getting back together, but she didn't want to lie to her, either. "I was with your dad."

Sam sat up and looked at her with big turquoise eyes. "You were?"

"Yeah. Remember, I went over there after I dropped you off so he could help me study for my test."

A dejected sigh escaped Samantha's lips. "Oh." She laid her head back down.

Jamie kissed her forehead. "Listen, baby. Don't get any ideas about me and your dad, okay? I don't know what's going to happen and I think you shouldn't get your hopes up that we will get back together." Tears threatened behind her eyes again when she remembered the night before in his arms.

"But you like him, don't you?"

"It's not that easy, baby."

"You loved him when you had me, right?"

Jamie's heart clenched in her chest before she answered, "Yeah baby, I did."

"You don't anymore?" The hope in Samantha's voice made her feel like crap. Sam wanted her mother and father to love each other again, just like any kid whose parents weren't together.

Jamie brushed the hair off Samantha's forehead. "I'm not sure what's between us now. We are different people than we were back then. He's been seeing other people."

Samantha's head came up again. "You mean he has a girlfriend?"

"I'm not sure what you would call it. You'll have to ask him that one."

"Humpf", left Samantha's lips. "Well, I know he likes you," Samantha said as she lay her head back down.

Jamie chuckled softly. "And how do you know that?"

"The way he looks at you. He does it a lot when you aren't looking, but I saw it yesterday at the party."

"Did you."

"Yeah. He kept watching you when he was cooking the hamburgers."

Jamie giggled and asked, "And what look would that be?"

"Like he wants to have sex with you."

"Samantha!" Jamie exclaimed as she moved so she could see her daughter's face. "How would you know what look that is?"

Samantha rolled her eyes. "Oh, Mom, you know." She sighed before she continued, "The look that says he would like to eat you for lunch. Or kiss you until you can't breathe. It's the kind of look I hope my husband will give me some day."

Jamie's breath left her lungs in a rush. She knew the look Samantha talked about. He had looked at her like that last night when he slipped his hard length inside her.

Good Lord! The man can make me cum for him with little more a kiss or a touch. She frowned. *Maybe I should have given him the benefit of the doubt and not rushed out. After all, I can't expect him to have been celibate for the last nine years.*

"Mom?"

"Yeah, sweetie."

"How come you were crying when I came in?"

"I had a little bit of a fight with your dad earlier."

"A fight? What kind of a fight?"

"It's something he and I need to talk about before I say anything more. More like a misunderstanding, but it had to do with him seeing other people."

"And that made you cry?"

"Yes."

"Are you jealous?"

Am I? Is that what these feelings are? Jealousy?

"Maybe just a little."

"Then you do love him," Samantha said in a matter-of-fact tone that broached no argument.

"If it were only that easy, baby. If it were only that easy."

Chapter Ten

The neon sign of Cowboy Lights glared in the fading sunlight when Jamie pulled her truck into an open parking space. It had been a week since she'd spent the night with Wyatt and she hadn't told a soul. Tonight she wanted to relax and get rip-roaring drunk, maybe find a cute cowboy to dance with and forget about the man who haunted her dreams.

"Hey, girl," Liz greeted her when she slid into their customary booth.

"What's going on?" Jamie asked, her eyes scanning the bar.

"Nothing. How about you? Seen Wyatt lately?"

Jamie shook her head and sighed. "You just don't give up, do you?"

"What?"

"Maybe Wyatt and I aren't seeing each other, you know?"

"Yeah—right." She nodded in the direction of the bar and said, "That's why his eyes have been glued to you since you walked in."

Jamie's head snapped around only to meet the piercing blue eyes of the man who made her heart stop in her chest. She turned back and faced Liz, intent on ignoring him completely.

Damn it! Why does he have to be here?

"Give it up, Jamie. You won't be able to ignore him all night. The sparks between you two are almost visible." Liz took a long drink of her beer. "Besides, the way that man eats you up with his eyes, I sure in the hell wouldn't be denying him or myself."

"There isn't anything between us."

"Then why are you blushing?"

Jamie put her hands to her cheeks before she said, "I am not."

"Yes you are. One look from those blue eyes of his and your whole body burns."

How the hell does she know? "Liz...you've never...I mean, you haven't..." Jamie's voice trailed off when her eyes focused on the scarred tabletop beneath her hand for a moment.

Liz looked at her curiously and then burst out laughing. "Have I ever been with Wyatt?"

"Yeah."

"Hell, no! Not like I wouldn't have if he had asked, but he's not interested in anyone but you, babe." Liz tipped the bottle to her lips again and then continued, "Besides, there are plenty of leftovers for me in here."

She swept her arm over the back of the booth and one blonde cowboy in the seat behind her leaned over. "That's right, baby. I'm sure I can make you scream."

Liz turned and gave him a provocative look as she replied, "I bet you can, honey."

"Liz!"

"What? I'm free, white and twenty-one. I can go home with whoever catches my fancy."

Jamie rolled her eyes and shook her head. "I don't believe you sometimes. Aren't you worried about catching something or getting pregnant?"

Liz wiped her mouth and pointed at Jamie as she said, "Listen, that's what condoms are for and the pill."

"But they don't always work."

"I'll take my chances, honey." Liz shot a glance over the back of the booth at the cowboy and smiled.

A moment later, Liz's gaze shot over the top of Jamie's head and she cocked a questioning eyebrow. Somehow, Jamie knew exactly who stood behind her, even if her whole body hadn't started to tingle when he moved close.

Wyatt's deep, slightly gravelly voice sent shivers down her arms when he asked, "Would you dance with me, Jamie?"

She turned and let her gaze wander up his chest before she focused on his blue eyes.

Damn! The man can curl my toes without even touching me.

Jamie tried to shrug nonchalantly, but she thought it looked more like she leaned toward him in anticipation. "I guess so." She stood and he placed his warm hand against the small of her back as she walked toward the dance floor.

The song changed from a two-step to a slow waltz and she tried not to grimace. The last thing she needed was for him to hold her close. Finally, she allowed him to slide one hand around her waist as she placed her hand in his. He cupped the hand he held with his own and brought it to his chest so their entwined hands rested against the muscles beneath his shirt.

She tried to pull back, but he held her tight and said, "You don't want to make a scene, do you?"

"I don't really care if I do or not, Wyatt. You should know enough about me to guess that." She tugged again, but not very forcibly.

"You don't like it when I hold you."

A frown pulled down the corners of her mouth. "It's not that I don't like it, it's just..." Lips firmed into a straight line when she clamped her mouth shut.

"Just what?" He tugged her closer and fit their bodies together like a jigsaw puzzle. "Just that you can't forget how I make you feel? How much you want me to make love to you again? That you miss my touch—my kiss..."

"Not the least bit conceited, are you?"

"Conceited?" Wyatt chuckled softly, his warm breath flittering across her cheek. "Conceit has nothing to do with it. I know how I feel when you are in my arms and I know the way your body molds to mine as if it were made to. You can't deny what it's like when we make love."

"Make love?" She shook her head in denial. "Have sex, yes— make love…" Flipping her hair over her shoulder, she continued, "We haven't made love in nine years, Wyatt."

Wyatt's lips skimmed her cheek before they stopped near her ear. "If you want to think of what happened between us since I've been back as having sex, so be it. I know I made love to you, whether you want to believe that or not."

The melody of the song changed, but he didn't let her go as they continued to sway slowly to the music. His lips moved down below her ear and followed the curve of her throat as she fought the urge to arch her neck to his touch.

"Come home with me. I need to love you."

Her body melted at his words, but her head screamed, *what about his dalliance two weeks ago?* "What's the matter? Can't get in touch with Amanda?"

He lifted his head as his eyes searched hers. "Huh?"

Jamie cocked her head slightly and said, "You know. The friend your neighbor mentioned."

A cocky smile rippled across his lips. "What's the matter? Jealous?"

She replied quickly, "No."

"Mmm…I think you are a liar, Jamie Wilder." The swayed for several heart-stopping seconds while their gazes held in a silent battle of wills. "It doesn't matter, you know. She was lying."

"Lying?"

"Yes. I haven't had anyone to my house since I moved in—no one except you, that is." A small smile appeared on his mouth. "But I like the fact that you don't want me with anyone else."

"I never said that."

"You didn't have to."

"Samantha wants us back together, you know," she said, but almost kicked herself for revealing that fact to him.

His gaze moved to her mouth and she licked her parched lips.

"So do I," he murmured when his gaze returned to hers. "What about you? Do you want us back together?"

"I can't think about that right now, Wyatt. I need to concentrate on passing my test and getting out on my own. The last thing I need is to become dependent on someone else, like I've been with my family."

Frown lines appeared between his eyes. "Dependent? Is that what you think you would be with me?"

"Yes. I need to prove it to myself that I can make it on my own. I haven't been able to do that."

Wyatt's shoulder lifted in a shrug. "Okay. How about we date?"

"What? You can't be serious?"

"Why not?"

"You want to date me."

"Yes. You said before, we've both changed over the years and that I don't know you anymore. Well, let me get to know you again."

Jamie chewed her bottom lip nervously. Being around him played havoc with her heart, but could she date him? Could they take a step back and just get to know each other again? What if she fell in love with him?

Not like I'm not already halfway there.

"How would that work?"

"You know, just date. We'll go out to dinner—to the movies—whatever."

"No kissing, no touching and no sex?"

Wyatt smiled mischievously. "Not right away, anyway."

"I don't do those things on the first date, you know."

"I distinctly remember that part of your personality." She knew indecision rippled across her features when he said, "Come on, Jamie. Give it a try—give us a try."

"All right, but we are going to take this slow. No rushing me, Wyatt. You promise?"

"Cross my heart."

"So how is this going to work?"

"What if I pick you up at your parent's house tomorrow evening since I don't have to work and we'll just go to dinner somewhere and then maybe to a movie?"

Her eyes focused on his throat a second, before they returned to his and she replied, "I guess that would be okay."

"When do you take your nursing test again?"

"Day after tomorrow, so we'll have to put off the dinner and movie until that's over. I have to be able to concentrate."

He cocked an eyebrow and asked, "Are you saying you can't concentrate with me around?"

"You do make it rather difficult, you know."

A half-crooked smile lifted the corners of his mouth.

Shit. I should never have told him that.

"Mmm...well I guess I'll just have to leave you alone until Monday night then."

"Yes, you will. In fact, I should head for home now so I can study."

They stepped apart and his hand found the small of her back as he escorted her back to the table to say goodbye to Liz. "Will you at least let me walk you out to your truck?"

"I guess. You know, I really planned on getting roaring drunk tonight so I could forget all about you."

"Did you?"

"Yes I did, but since we're dating now, I guess that's probably a moot point."

"Probably."

The question on the face of her 'friend' almost had her smiling. "Liz, I'm heading home."

"With Wyatt?"

"Noooo..." She felt like slapping that smirk on Liz's face. "I'm going back to my parents so I can study. I'll see you later."

"Sure, girl. Don't do anything I wouldn't do."

Jamie rolled her eyes. "I know what you would do, Liz, and no, I'm not going there." After she grabbed her purse, she turned to Wyatt and said, "Shall we go?"

"After you, pretty lady."

She shook her head and turned toward the entrance with Wyatt's hand caressing the small of her back.

"I thought there was no touching?"

"At least give me this much, Jamie. How about no touching after tonight?" He grinned and she sighed.

Wyatt's bike sat a few feet from the door and when they stopped next to it, she said, "You're impossible."

He wrapped his arms around her and pulled her close. "I know, but you love me anyway."

Her startled gaze fixed on him. *I hope it's not that obvious.* "I never said that."

Wyatt just smiled, before his lips found the corners of her mouth and nibbled softly. His tongue slipped along the crease of her lips and she sighed as she opened for him. He moaned when his tongue dove inside her mouth, dancing with her own for a moment. Wyatt's hand slipped into her hair and caressed the back of her head with his hand.

"I better go," she whispered.

"I know." He stepped back and dropped his hands. "I'm going to do the gentlemanly thing and let you go home without ravishing you first."

"If you don't, this dating thing won't work."

"You are such a hard-nose." He chuckle softly, leaned over and kissed her quickly on the lips. "I'll see you on Monday, then."

She stepped back as he straddled the bike, slipped on his helmet and hit the ignition. He brought up the kickstand and blew her a kiss before he pulled way.

Her fingers drifted to her lips as they tingled from the pressure of his mouth. She shook her head and smiled softly, before she pulled out her keys and headed for her truck.

When she finally reached the house, she headed for her room, the smile still lingering on her lips. She reached for the doorknob just as Samantha came out of hers.

"Hey, Mom. I thought you were going out tonight?"

"I did for a little bit, but I realized I should probably come home and study since my test is Monday. What are you still doing up?"

Samantha rolled her eyes. "It's Saturday, Mom."

Jamie tweaked her nose as she said, "That doesn't mean free rein to stay up until the wee hours."

"It's only ten."

"Yeah, well, you need your beauty sleep."

"Whatever." Samantha leaned over and sniffed her shirt, before she asked, "Was Dad at the bar?"

Jamie's startled gaze met her daughter's. "Why do you ask that?"

Samantha's shoulder lifted in a half shrug. "Your shirt smells like him."

"I can't get away with anything, can I?"

"He *was* there."

"Yes, Samantha, he was."

Samantha smiled and the dimples that branded her a Wilder, peeked out of her cheeks. "Did you dance with him?"

"Yes."

Their daughter pumped her fist as she squealed, "Yesss."

"Don't get your hopes up, young lady."

"At least you danced with him. It's a start."

"I'm going to bed now, Sam."

"You're avoiding talking to me about him, Mother, but that's okay. I can always call him and ask. He'll tell me." Sam grinned again.

Jamie set her hands on her hips as she tried to look sternly at Sam. "I obviously need to have a talk with your father."

"Night, Mom."

"Samantha Renee…"

Sam smiled and disappeared into her room as Jamie sighed heavily. She pushed open her own bedroom and quickly closed the door behind her before she stripped off her clothes and headed for the shower.

I need a nice, relaxing, hot shower and I'll sleep like a baby.

"That is until turquoise blue eyes invade my dreams," she grumbled as she turned on the water and slipped beneath the stream. Once she finished, she slid between the cool sheets on her bed and tried to close her eyes.

Several moments later, she rolled over and grabbed her cell phone from the nightstand. She flipped through the numbers until she found the one she sought and hit talk.

"Hey." The soft low rumble of his voice met her ear and she smiled.

God, I love the sound of his voice. Silky and sexy with the right amount of growl, exactly enough to set my panties on fire.

"Hi."

"Can't sleep?"

"Mmm...how'd you guess?"

She could almost hear the smile in his voice. "I don't think you've changed that much, baby. If I remember correctly, you used to do this quite a bit when we were younger."

"What's that?" she whispered.

"Call me when you couldn't sleep."

"Am I that transparent?"

"Only to me."

She sighed. "Did Sam call you?"

"Yeah. A little while ago. She said you told her we danced at the bar."

"She could smell you on my shirt."

His soft chuckle met her ear as he said, "I guess I'll have to change my cologne then."

"No...don't."

"Why?"

"I like your cologne."

Silence met her ear for several long moments.

"I wish I was there with you."

"I wish you were too," she murmured, before she sighed. "I guess I should go so I can try to get some sleep. I need to be rested for this test on Monday."

"You'll do fine, honey. I have confidence in you."

"Thanks, Wyatt. You always know exactly what to say."

"Sweet dreams, baby."

"Night."

* * * *

Jamie took a deep breath and stared at the computer screen in front of her. With shaking hands, she reached for the mouse and clicked the start button that would begin the test as she chewed her bottom lip. The first question popped up on the screen and she slowly read the entire thing before she clicked on an answer.

I can do this. I know I can do this.

Two hours later, she walked out of the classroom with a huge smile on her face. Her test had stopped at seventy-five questions and she felt confident that she had passed, even though she wouldn't know for sure until three days from now.

She quickly walked to her truck, pulled the keys and her cell phone from her purse before she opened the door and slid inside. Her finger flipped through the phonebook on her phone as she grinned from ear to ear and dialed.

"Hey. How'd it go?"

She chewed her bottom lip before she said, "Good—I think."

"What do you mean, you think?"

"Well…there are two hundred and sixty five questions, maximum on the test. Mine stopped at seventy five."

"Is that good or bad?"

"Depends."

"On?"

"Well, from what I've heard, if it stops at seventy five, you either did great and that's all it took for the computer to determine you passed or you did really bad and you failed miserably."

"I'm sure you passed with flying colors."

"God, I hope so Wyatt, but what if I didn't?"

"Then you'll take it again in a few months. Don't worry."

"I can't help it."

"Want me to take your mind off of it?"

She smiled to herself as she asked, "What do you have in mind?"

"We were supposed to do dinner and a movie tonight, but why don't you come over here and I'll cook."

She laughed. "You're going to cook?"

"Of course. I've learned several interesting things since we were together. How about you come over here and I'll show you."

Her pussy clenched at the thought, but she didn't think he meant 'interesting things' in the sexual department, or did he?

I'm the one that set down the rules of no kissing, no touching and definitely, no sex. Damn it anyway!

"I'll be there in thirty minutes."

"Make it an hour and I'll run to the store to get some things for dinner. How would you like chicken parmesan with a green salad and pasta?"

"Sounds yummy. Do you want me to bring anything?"

"Why don't you get a nice white wine, like Pinot Noir?"

"Perfect. I'll see you in a bit."

Jamie hung up the phone as she started the truck before she pulled out into the street and headed for home. She wanted a quick shower before she went to his place for dinner. When she reached the house, she almost skipped up the stairs to her room, only to be stopped by

Samantha as she stood against her door jamb, with her arms across her chest and a pleased smile on her lips.

"What are you grinning about, young lady?"

"Going to Dad's?"

Jamie frowned. Damn, she hated being so obvious. "Yes, if you must know."

"He said you two were dating."

I'm going to have to talk to him about discussing our relationship with Samantha. It wouldn't do any good to get her hopes up.

"Yeah, well, it's just dinner, Sam."

"It's a start, Mom." Samantha's grin widened enough that her dimples peeked out of her cheeks and she said, "Have a good time and don't worry about coming home."

"Samantha!"

Sam whistled softly as she disappeared down the hall and Jamie shook her head in disbelief. Jamie went inside her room and pulled out different clothing in an attempt to find something suitable to wear.

"No," she said, tossing aside the flowered top she held. She picked up a blue tank top with small straps that held it up at her shoulders and eyed it speculatively. Tapping her finger against her lip, she finally set it aside as she decided it would be the shirt she'd wear. "Now. Jeans? Skirt? Mmm…" She held up a pair of jeans, and then switched to the skirt, before she decided on the jeans. "Thong? Oh, yeah."

Chapter Eleven

One hour later, she rang the doorbell on his house and she smiled when she heard the music coming from inside. He knew her favorite music and he played on the fact as George Strait crooned "I Cross My Heart." She shook her head, smiled and looked at the toes of her boots when she remembered their first dance. They had taken a picnic out near the river and he'd brought along a radio. When that song came on, he asked her to dance with him under the trees. Her heart had hammered so hard, she'd thought it would jump right out of her chest.

The door whipped open and she peeked through her lashes at the man who had stolen her heart so many years before. Dressed in a button-up shirt and jeans, he looked like something wet dreams were made of, hers at least.

"You don't have to ring the doorbell," he said as he grasped her hand and pulled her inside, before he shut it behind her and pushed her against the door for a heart-stopping kiss. "Damn, you taste good."

Grabbing a fistful of his shirt, she kissed him quickly and replied, "It's not my house, Wyatt. I don't walk into other people's homes without knocking. My mother would have a coronary if I did."

Smack.

One hand came down on her butt cheek as his laughter reached her ears with a rich sound that rolled down her back and made her shiver. "Very true. Come on in."

She held out the brown paper sack. "Here's the wine."

"Great. Dinner will be ready in a little bit, but how about we start with that."

Cocking a questioning eyebrow, she asked, "Are you going to try to get me drunk?"

He grinned innocently. "Not me."

Wyatt moved toward the kitchen as she walked into the living room and took a seat on the couch. Her palms started to sweat when her gaze moved to the end and flashes of them making love there zipped across her mind. Wiping her hands down the thighs of her jeans, she took a deep breath in a vain attempt to calm her racing heart.

She jumped, startled when he stopped next to her and extended the glass of wine.

"Jumpy?"

The nervous laugh bubbling from her mouth, made her frown. The feelings of insecurity crowded her heart. "Yeah. Just a little."

"Why?"

"It's the whole dating thing, I guess. It kind of takes me back to when I was seventeen and our first date." Jamie took a sip of the wine and let the cool liquid slide down her throat, hoping it would cool her down and stop the tickle of sweat now rolling down her back. "My friends were so jealous."

Wyatt took the chair across from her as he took a drink of his own glass before he smiled. "Why?"

"I had a date with a college guy. It was a big deal to a bunch of teenage girls."

The warm smile that lifted the corners of his mouth, calmed her soul.

"I know our first date didn't consist of me cooking you dinner."

Jamie chuckled. "No—no it didn't."

"If I remember correctly, I picked you up at the ranch and we went for a picnic."

Tracing the rim of her wine goblet with her finger, she smiled at the memories. "And we ended up soaking wet when you pushed me in the pond."

"I didn't push you." Laugh lines creased the corners near his eyes as a grin settled on his mouth.

"You are such a liar, Wyatt. Yes, you did."

Eyes twinkled temptingly as he shook his head in denial. "No. We were sitting on the log, talking, and you fell in, but you took me with you so we were both soaking wet." A chuckle fell from his lips and the deep sound sent her heart into overdrive. "Your mom had a fit. She thought for sure I had taken advantage of you."

"That would have been impossible at the time. My jeans were so tight; you would have played hell getting them off, much less with them being wet."

"They were. Tight I mean. You have such a nice ass in tight jeans."

"Is that supposed to be an off-handed compliment?" She sipped at the wine again, feeling a slight buzz as her head swam a little.

"Take it how you want. I don't deny I love your butt in jeans," his gaze swept down her chest before they returned to hers and he continued, "or out."

She closed her eyes, bit her lower lip and sighed.

Damn, he's making this hard.

Wyatt took a sip of his wine and stood. "I'll be right back. Dinner should be ready."

"Would you like some help? I make a mean green salad."

He grinned and said, "Sure."

Following him into the kitchen, her stomach growled as the scent of chicken, spaghetti sauce, garlic and cheese reached her nose. "That smells heavenly. When did you learn to cook?"

Wyatt stirred the pasta on the stove a minute before he opened the refrigerator and pulled out the lettuce, tomato, cucumber and salad dressings. He set everything on the counter before his eyes swept back to her. "I got tired of eating out during medical school. You can only eat so much McDonald's, Taco Bell and all that stuff. It gets old after awhile."

"I can imagine." Jamie unwrapped the lettuce, removed the core and asked, "Knife?"

"In the drawer there next to you." He stirred the pasta again before he grabbed the strainer, set it in the sink and dumped the noodles inside.

Grabbing a large butcher knife, she efficiently cut all the ingredients and put them in the bowl he set near her elbow.

They worked in compatible silence as he dished up the food onto plates and nodded with his head, indicating she should move back toward the dining room with the salad. He set each plate down and that's when she noticed the intimate setting he had created. Candlelight reflected off the silverware and crystal glasses sitting on the tabletop. A cool summer breeze ruffled the curtains on the window nearby and the sweet scent of honeysuckle drifted inside.

Jamie set the bowl on the corner of the table while Wyatt pulled out the chair for her to sit. Once she sat comfortably, his whispered words caressed the side of her neck and sent desire zinging along her nerve endings to settle between her thighs.

"I love the way you smell. Did you wear that perfume on purpose?"

He moved from behind her and took his own chair as a devilish smile settled on his oh-so-kissable lips.

"No." His eyebrow rose in disbelief. "All right, yes. I knew it used to be your favorite."

"Still is," he said as he grasped her hand in his.

"I thought we said no touching?"

Why the hell did I say that? I know I want him to touch me, kiss me, and make love to me. Stupid.

He let go and frowned. "I didn't think that meant I couldn't touch you at all, but if that's the way you want it…" Picking up his fork and knife, he cut the tender chicken and stuck a piece in his mouth.

Great! Now he's going to ignore me.

He surprised her by saying, "Have you been to the doctor?"

"About?"

The concern returned to his gaze as it focused on her face. "Your headaches and passing out?"

She sighed and looked at her own meal. "No."

His fork clanked to the plate, bringing her startled eyes back to his as he exclaimed, "Damn it, Jamie!"

"What?"

"Are you just hoping nothing is wrong or are you really that damned stubborn?"

"I'm fine, Wyatt. I haven't had any more spells in a couple of weeks."

"That doesn't mean the whole thing has gone away. Will you please listen to me and go see a doctor, preferably a neurologist?"

"So they can do what, exactly?

He ran his hand through his hair in frustration before he pinned her to her chair with his gaze. "Run some tests, do an exam."

"Will it make you feel better if I do?"

Wyatt grasped her hand and squeezed. "Yes. I'm worried about you, baby. These symptoms aren't normal."

"All right. I'll call and make an appointment with someone tomorrow."

He sighed in relief. "Good."

She bit her lip nervously for a moment before she asked, "Will you go with me? I mean, you can help me interpret what they say."

Wyatt kissed the palm he held before he replied, "Of course. Just let me know what date you set it up for and we'll go together."

"Can we get on with this date now and leave all this serious talk behind?"

"What did you have in mind?" His eyes sparkled with a promise she wanted to accept.

I wonder if I can convince him to forget the no touching—no sex stipulation.

"How about we finish eating and watch a movie on the couch?"

"There is probably something in my collection you haven't seen, unless you would rather go to the theatre."

She shrugged and stuffed a forkful of food in her mouth. "I haven't been to a movie theatre in a long time."

"All right, then. When we've finished eating, I'll do up the dishes and you can pick something from the listings in the newspaper."

"I'll do the dishes."

He shook his head. "No, you won't. I invited you for dinner, I'll do the dishes."

"But you cooked. At least I can clean up."

"I tell you what. We can do them together. I'll rinse and you can load them in the dishwasher. Then we'll figure out what we want to go see."

"Sounds good to me."

Once they had finished eating, they retreated to the kitchen with their plates and quickly cleaned up.

"The paper is there on the counter if you want to look to see what is playing while I wipe the stove off."

"Okay." Jamie grabbed the newspaper and flipped it open to the movie listings, skimming it with her finger as she bit her lip in concentration. A moment later, he moved behind her a peered over her shoulder.

"Anything catch your eye?"

She peeked over her shoulder at the gorgeous man resting against her back and sighed.

Oh, yeah. You.

Her attention returned to the movie listings as she said, "Let's see. Do we want action film, romantic, or horror?"

"What about a scary movie? That way when you get scared you can cuddle up to me."

"Ah…ulterior motive. I like it!" He grinned and she turned around, looped her arms around his neck as his hands settled on her hips and placed a quick kiss to his mouth.

Wyatt growled low in his throat and his hands tightened on her waist. "I thought you said no touching and no kissing on this date?"

She let a teasing smile lift the corners of her mouth. "Maybe I changed my mind? Besides, we are both adults, right? I think we can handle being together with a touch or kiss."

"What about the no sex?"

"That will have to be negotiated."

He nuzzled her neck and she sighed as he whispered against her skin, "I'm good at negotiations." His fingers slipped up her side and settled beneath her breast.

Jamie's breath came out in a rush of air when his palm settled over the soft flesh of her breast.

God, I love it when he touches me.

"We won't be getting to the movies if you keep that up."

Wyatt lifted his head and smiled. "We could make our own movie?"

She gasped in surprise. "Wyatt! I am *not* making any kind of movie with you." His rich deep laughter sent chills down her spine. Jamie pushed him back and punched him in the shoulder. "*You* are impossible!"

"What? It was only a suggestion." He chuckled as he tried to nuzzle her neck again, but she slipped out of his embrace and headed for the living room, with him on her heels.

"A suggestion we aren't going to pursue right now, mister." She grabbed her purse and slung it over her shoulder as she tapped her foot and shot him a teasing glance.

He grabbed his keys off the end table. "We can take my bike or my car."

"How about the Harley? I've never been on one."

Wyatt gave her a sexy grin before he wrapped an arm around her waist and pulled her close for a kiss. "I think I like the thought of your arms around my waist, your legs cradling me…"

"You make riding your bike sound sexy as hell," she whispered.

"I think you'll like the power between your legs."

She wasn't sure if he meant the bike's power or his own, but both made her panties wet.

This no sex thing just isn't going to work. I can't be in the same room with him without wanting to feel him deep inside me.

"I can't wait," she murmured, shooting him a teasing glance from beneath her eyelashes.

"You are a serious tease, Jamie Wilder," he growled in pretend fierceness.

Her eyes widened in mock surprise. "Who, me?"

"Yes, you, woman. You have no idea how much I want to bury myself inside you right now." His hands grasped her ass cheeks and pulled her tight against his groin.

Her fingers found his chest and skimmed down the hard muscles under her palm. "Sounds promising."

"Jamie," he whispered. "God, I want you."

She smiled and stepped back. "We have a movie to attend."

"Brat."

"I'm sure I can make it up to you…later."

"Is that a promise or a threat?"

"Take it however you prefer, Doctor Crossland."

"This better be a damned short movie."

She spun on her heel and laughed all the way out the door.

* * * *

A few hours later, after a two-hour movie, a dessert stop at Baskin Robbins for ice cream and a quick run into the grocery store for whipped cream, Jamie and Wyatt reached his house. Her tongue had teased along the part of his neck exposed under his helmet and her fingers had danced along his abdomen the entire ride back. His cock pressed hard against the fly of his jeans and he thought for sure his head would explode from the roar of blood in his ears before they got back. He couldn't wait to taste the cool, sweet flavor of whipped cream against her skin.

Wyatt turned the bike off and set the kickstand down before Jamie scooted off the back. She pulled the helmet off and shook her head before her hair settled in waves on her shoulders.

I love her hair.

It was all he could do to keep from throwing her over his shoulder and running for the house.

"You got the bag?"

Smiling, she held up the brown paper sack and answered, "Yep."

"Good." He grabbed her hand and almost pulled her arm out of the socket in the rush to get her inside. "Let's go."

Giggling softly, she said, "Are you in a hurry, Wyatt?"

"Damned right! I'm horny as the devil and you've been teasing me since you walked into my house before supper. Making love to you once every couple of weeks is torture, you know."

"You don't think I'm there too? It's not like I have a steady stream of men waiting in the wings to take care of my problem."

"That's a good thing. I won't have to hurt anyone then," he grumbled as he pushed open the door.

They made it as far as the kitchen, before he pinned her against the counter and his mouth captured hers in a desperate kiss. His tongue slipped between her half-parted lips. He caught her moan in his mouth when his hand pulled the thin straps of her shirt down to reveal her breasts. He pulled his mouth away and slid his lips along her cheek until he reached her ear. Nibbling on her earlobe, he felt a shiver roll down her body as the goose bumps rippled along her skin. His fingers flicked the button on her jeans free before he found the zipper and yanked it down. One hand slid down her flat stomach, under the waistband of her underwear to slide through the curls before one finger rasped along her clit. Her legs widened as she groaned her pleasure.

"Need. To. Get. These. Off," he growled against her neck while his hands worked around the back of her jeans. He chuckled softly when his hands met her bare ass. "God, I love thongs."

"Good. Now get it off. I want to feel your mouth," she murmured.

He growled as he pushed her jeans down along with her sexy underwear until they pooled at her feet. She kicked them loose and he lifted her until her butt met the cool countertop.

"Damn, that's cold."

He alternated between licking and sucking at the hardened nipple while she wiggled her butt, trying to get closer.

"Wyatt, please."

"Please what?"

"Eat me, fuck me, do something! I need…Oh, God!"

His mouth settled on her clit. While he sucked it into his mouth, he slid two fingers, knuckle deep inside her hot center. Cream spilled from her pussy as she grasped his head in her hands.

He lapped at her until she stopped shivering from her climax and then he kissed his way up her stomach. When he reached her mouth, his tongue dove inside as his fingers rolled her nipple.

Her hand wrapped around his stiff cock and he groaned low in his throat. With her palm doing a slow slide up and down while he rocked his hips toward her, she swore he grew bigger within her grasp. He moved far enough back, and she hopped off the countertop so she could reach his chest with her lips. She nipped at his nipple before she licked the hard nub and his skin quivered under her touch.

"Jamie," he growled.

"Mmm…" Her mouth moved down his chest, following the line of hair that ended at his groin. She dropped to her knees and her mouth wrapped around the head of his penis, taking him within her warmth.

"Ah. God," he panted as he thread his fingers in her hair and held her head in place. He rocked in time with the slide of her lips and her tongue. "If. You. Don't. Stop…I'm gonna come, baby."

She grabbed his ass with both hands and held him in place as she continued to suck everything he had. His balls drew up tight and he felt the unmistakable roar of his climax zing from his toes to settle at the base of his cock. A groan rumbled in his chest and burst from his lips when come shot to the back of her throat. She sucked and swallowed until he had nothing left. When she finally let his softening cock slip from between her lips, she stood in front of him with a wicked smile on her mouth.

"I hope you aren't a one-shot wonder."

He tossed his head back and laughed. "Not on your life, baby." Lifting her in his arms, she squealed when he headed down the hall to his bedroom and kept walking until he reached the bathroom.

"The shower?" she asked, with delight dancing in her brown eyes.

"You bet," he said as he reached over the turned on the spray.

"This should be fun. I haven't done this in a long time." She stepped into the shower stall and let the warm water sluice down her chest. "Are you going to join me?"

"Oh. Yeah." He walked inside and pulled the shower door closed behind him. Reaching for her breasts, he cupped the mounds in his hands, letting his palms slide over her already hard nipples. "I love your breasts. They fit perfectly in my hands." He bent down and took the tip in his mouth and sucked softly while his fingers pinched and rolled its mate.

Her wet hand sifted through the curls at the back of his head and held him tight against her chest as she moaned her delight. "God, Wyatt. What you do to me drives me crazy."

His left hand skimmed down her belly to slide between her pussy lips and delve into her hot warmth. She whimpered and rocked her hips with the movement of his fingers.

Forcing him to stop his wicked torture with a quick step backwards, she gave him a teasing smile, found the soap and began to lather her hands.

He stepped back slightly while her slippery hands moved over his chest, down his abdomen and cupped his balls. Groaning his pleasure at the slide of her hands, he rocked his hips as he felt the blood rush back to his cock.

Good lord, what she does to me.

"Like that?"

"Oh, hell yes."

A dimpled smile graced her lips and he swore he'd died and gone to heaven. "Jamie," he growled, grasping her hands to stop her torturous fondling. "I'm hard as a damned rock, baby. Keep that up and this is going to be a quick trip."

"Don't want that now, do we?"

"No, we don't."

"Is there a condom in here?"

He pushed open the shower door, reached into the drawer of the vanity and pulled out the foil package before he handed it to her and shut the door again. His breath came out in a rush as she grasped his cock and slid the latex over his shaft.

Presenting him with her back, she bent over at the waist, shot him a saucy smile over her shoulder and spread her thighs as she murmured, "Fuck me, Wyatt. Now—right now."

"God, Jamie," he growled as he positioned himself at her opening and pushed inside as deep as he could. He grasped her hips and rocked his groin against her ass. "You feel like heaven."

A soft whimper left her lips as she pushed back against him. He could feel her vagina squeezing him and holding him within her soft walls as he moved. The warm water cascaded over her ass and rolled down between them as he pistoned inside her until she climaxed around him and screamed his name. He roared his own completion moments after her.

They stayed joined for a couple of minutes as they tried to catch their breath, until he finally slipped from her warmth.

He grabbed the soap and lathered some between his hands as he grinned and said, "Now. I get to play."

Chapter Twelve

Wyatt walked into the emergency room with a silly grin on his face and a whistle on his lips. His new relationship with Jamie had taken on a life of its own. Ever since they agreed to start dating, the two of them had spent many an afternoon together and on into the night. Making love to her had taken on a whole new meaning with the feelings swelling in his heart. He knew he loved her nine years ago, but what he felt now seemed to encompass his entire soul and he wanted nothing more than to spend the rest of his life with her.

"Good morning, people! How are all of you this fine, glorious morning?"

That earned him a grumble and a few raised eyebrows as he swept past the nurse's station and headed for the doctor's lounge to store his duffle.

He stuffed his bag into his locker, grabbed his stethoscope and headed back the way he had come.

When he rounded the corner of the counter, Stacy asked, "What are you so chipper this morning for, doc?"

A wide grin spread across his face as he shrugged, "Nothing. It's just a beautiful day."

Four heads tipped to the left and peeked out the window at the rain cutting sideways across the parking lot.

"It's raining cats and dogs out there and you think it's beautiful?" Marty asked.

"Everything is beautiful when one is in love," Angela said with a grin.

"Yeah, whatever," Amy grumbled as she stood propped against the counter.

Wyatt looked at Amy and her eyes narrowed when they raked down his chest and settled on his groin, before returning to his face.

Damn, she's bold!

His gaze returned to the others at the desk and he said, "I'm not saying a word." He tapped Doctor Hamilton on the shoulder to get his attention and he got a quick report on the patients needing his concentration at the moment.

Wyatt grabbed a chart and headed for the first exam room.

A few hours later, the cell phone clipped to his belt rang and when he looked at the screen, a wide smile spread across his face before he answered. "Hey, babe."

"Are you busy?"

"Not too busy for you. What's up?"

"I wanted to remind you of my appointment with the neurologist. I know how forgetful you can be."

"When is it again?"

"Day after tomorrow. Put it in your calendar, Wyatt, so you don't forget."

"Yes, ma'am." He wrote down the date and time. "Aren't you working today?"

"Yeah. I'm upstairs, but I'll be getting lunch soon. Do you want to meet me in the cafeteria?"

"Sure. The patients have slowed down a bit so I can take a break. How about in thirty minutes?"

"Perfect. I'll see you shortly."

"Bye, babe."

"Bye."

Thirty minutes later found him and Jamie in a corner booth in the cafeteria sharing lunch. He took her hand in his and kissed her palm. Pink colored her cheeks as she pulled it back. "You need to stop doing that. We're at work."

"What we do on our lunch break is our time. It's not like I pushed you into a supply closet and had my way with you, although I kind of like that idea."

"Wyatt!" Jamie whispered low. A few pairs of eyes fixed on them and she picked up her sandwich to hide her embarrassment.

He chuckled softly and picked up his fork. "I can't help how I feel so you might as well get used to the idea."

She rolled her eyes and changed the subject. "Did you put my appointment in your calendar?"

"Yes, ma'am, I did." He took a bite of his mashed potatoes. "Are you coming over tonight?"

"I can't."

"Why not?"

"Samantha is having a sleepover tonight and I can't leave my mother with three giggling preteen girls. Besides, I need to spend some extra time with Sam."

Frown lines creased his forehead. "Why?"

Jamie's shoulder lifted in a shrug. "I think she's feeling a bit neglected lately, with us spending so much time together." She stuck a chip in her mouth before she continued, "Don't get me wrong. She loves that we're together, but she doesn't see me as much and I don't want her to feel like I've chosen you over her."

"How about we do a family thing tomorrow after her friends go home? You are off for the next couple of days, right?"

"Yes."

"Great. So am I. How about we go camping? We can pitch a tent, roast marshmallows, have a campfire—you know those family things." He picked up her hand and kissed her fingertips. "I'll miss having you with me tonight though, too."

She groaned softly and retrieved her hand. Her face lit up with a smile that made his heart pound in his chest and she tapped her fingertip to her lips. "Why don't we take a couple of horses from Chase's place and go out by the river where we used to go when we were younger? We can still pitch a tent and stuff, we'll just camp out with the horses instead of a car."

"Sounds like fun, although you and Sam will have to cut me some slack. I haven't been on a horse in a number of years. I know I'm pretty rusty at it."

"It's like riding a bike—you never forget." She glanced at her watch. "Oops. Back to work. I'll call you tomorrow morning and we can arrange to meet somewhere."

"Sure," he said as they slid out of the booth and placed their trays on the conveyer belt. They walked to the elevator and he pushed the button for her. He shot her a sideways glance as the ping of the elevator indicated it would be arriving shortly. Turning his head from side to side to check for anyone watching, he leaned down and quickly kissed her on the lips. "Talk to you later." He walked away with a smile as her mouth opened and closed.

* * * *

"Hey, beautiful." Jamie smiled wistfully to herself as his words reached her ear through the phone. She lay across her bed on her stomach and slowly kicked her feet. "Lonely?"

"I'd much rather be in your company than listening to our daughter and her friends giggling in the other room."

"Me too, but your mom needs you there."

A sigh rushed from her lips. "I know. I have to be the responsible adult, but that doesn't mean I can't call and talk to you on the phone for awhile."

"Very true."

Silence stretched over the phone line for a moment before he said, "What would you like to talk about?"

"Welll…we could do what we used to do when we were younger."

"Jamie," he growled softly into the phone. "If you are suggesting what I think you are suggesting…you're a witch."

"What? Are you going to complain? You used to enjoy it when we did it before."

"I would much rather be having real sex with you instead of phone sex."

"Yes, but that's not possible tonight, so are you going to play along or do I have to imagine you licking my pussy all by myself?" A low rumble met her ear and she smiled. "Is that a yes?"

"What are you doing right now?"

"Sliding my pants and underwear off."

"What kind of underwear are you wearing?"

"That silky thong you like so much. You know—the black one."

"Are you sliding your fingers across your pussy lips as you take them off?"

"Oh, yeah." She moaned softly. "They are filled and aching for your mouth."

"God, Jamie."

"Do you have your cock in your hand?"

"Yes," he growled.

"Stroke it for me. Imagine my hot, wet lips sliding over the end as I take you in my mouth." His ragged breath met her ear and she closed her eyes as her middle finger found her clit. "Mmm…"

"Are you playing with your clit?"

She groaned.

"Toggle it for me, baby. Feel my tongue?"

"Oh, God!"

"Are you close?"

She whimpered as she continued to rub her clit harder and harder.

"I'm there with you, baby. I love the way you taste. Come with me." His gravelly, rough voice sent her over the edge as she felt her climax race up her legs and settle in her groin. She clamped her lips together as she moaned. She heard his cry of completion in her ear when her body quivered and shook.

After a minute or two of ragged breathing, she giggled and said, "Was it good for you?"

"Not as good as if you were here, but I guess it will have to do until tomorrow."

"I guess so." She stood up and slipped her pajama bottoms on. "I better go check on the girls. They're awfully quiet in there."

"Okay. I have a couple of charts I need to work on, anyway."

She wanted to say 'I love you' so bad her heart ached, but instead she said, "I'll call you in the morning."

"Sure. Don't let those girls get to you. Just remember, you were that age once, too." His soft chuckle met her ear as she tucked a piece of hair out of the way.

"I know. I just don't want them staying up too late. I'll see you tomorrow."

"Sweet dreams."

"Mmm…after our little foreplay, I just might."

* * * *

Wyatt stood in the living room of the Rocking W as Abby shot him a speculative look.

"Is there something you want to say, Abby?"

She shook her head and gave him a knowing grin as she said, "Nope."

"Where's Chase?"

"Out in the barn," she answered as Jeremiah giggled and ran around her legs. She grabbed him and picked him up in her arms. "Naptime for you, little man."

"I'm going to head out there and have him pick out a horse for me, since I haven't been on one in a long time. Hopefully, he won't give me one that will take off with me and kill me in the process. I know he doesn't like me too well."

"It's not that, Wyatt. He's just protective of Jamie and he isn't quite sure you two being together is the best thing for her."

He scowled. "Jamie and I are going to be together for a long time to come, so he'll just have to get used to it."

She smiled and shook her head. "He's stubborn and bullheaded."

"Tell me something I don't know."

"He loves her and doesn't want to see her hurt."

"I'm not going to her hurt."

"I know that, but he doesn't."

"What do you mean, Abby?"

"I don't know if Jamie told you about me, but I can see things— feel things, and I know you and Jamie are meant to be together. Chase doesn't see that yet. He's been protecting her for awhile now—nine years to be exact, and even though she's explained to him how things went down, he is still mad that you gave up and left town."

"I've explained why I left."

"It doesn't mean he's accepted it, Wyatt. I think he's holding out judgment until he sees for himself you aren't going to pack up and go again."

"I won't leave Jamie and Samantha. If I had to go somewhere else for some reason, I would take them with me."

"I'm happy to hear that."

"So am I," Chase said from behind Wyatt.

Wyatt spun around to face Jamie's brother. "Chase."

Abby moved to her husband's side and kissed him quickly on the lips. "I'm going to take Jeremiah into his room. I think you two need to talk."

Once she disappeared down the hall, Chase took a seat in the leather armchair in front of the cold fireplace. "Have a seat, Wyatt."

Gingerly, Wyatt took his place on the couch and watched Chase over the coffee table.

"What are your intentions with my sister?"

"I think that's between her and I, don't you?"

"No. Justin, Cole and I want to know what your plan is for the future."

"You aren't going to scare me into leaving her alone. I love her and I want to spend the rest of my life with her."

"Does she know this?"

"I think so, but I haven't asked her to marry me—yet."

"Do you intend to?"

"Yes."

The radio at Chase's belt crackled. "Accident at Hwy 210 and West Pilot Peak Road. Injuries."

Abby burst into the living room from Jeremiah's room. Her face was pasty white and it brought Chase to his feet as he wrapped her in his arms. "What's wrong?"

Her voice broke as she stammered, "It's Jamie."

Wyatt sprang to his feet. "What do you mean, it's Jamie?"

"The accident." Her eyes bored into his and his heart slammed against his ribs. "It's Jamie."

"You stay here, baby. I'll let you know what's going on as soon as I know," Chase whispered, before he kissed her quickly and grabbed his keys.

"I'm coming along," Wyatt said as he followed Chase out of the house.

"You'll be in the way," Chase grumbled.

"Damn it, Chase! Even if it's not Jamie, I'm a doctor, for crying out loud! I can help."

"Fine. Get in the truck."

The rode in silence until they came up on the accident. At first, he couldn't see the truck, but when they scrambled out of the cab, his heart dropped into his toes. A semi truck sat cross-ways in the intersection and the front end of a black pickup was crushed under the trailer.

Wyatt couldn't tell if the truck belonged to Jamie or not, but as he approached the driver's side, he could see her. "Oh, God," he whispered. "Please lord, please let her be okay."

"Jamie! Jamie, baby, wake up." Her chest rose and fell with her breathing and he sent up a silent thank you, knowing she was at least alive.

Chase slid inside the passenger side door, across the seat and wrapped his hands around her neck to stabilize her.

"She's breathing, right?"

"Yeah, but I don't like the look of how her chest is rising. It's not symmetrical."

"Shit! Is she only breathing on one side of her chest?"

"Appears so."

"I need to get in there."

"Just stay where you are, Wyatt. You can't do anything in here anyway." Sirens blared in the distance as help got closer. "The rest of them will be here shortly and once we get her out, you can see what you can do."

Shortly afterward, the fire trucks and ambulances arrived and one of the EMT's said, "Hey doc. Just happened to be in the neighborhood?"

"Yeah—you could say that." He raked his fingers through his hair and then growled, "Get that damned door open!"

"Patience, doc."

"I don't have patience right now. That's the woman I love in there."

Eyebrows shot up in surprise, but no one said anything as they worked quickly to get her out. Once he could reach her, he grabbed one of the stethoscopes from the paramedic and listened to her chest.

"Fuck!"

"What?" Chase asked.

"She's probably got a punctured lung. I'm not hearing anything on her right side." He looked at the EMT standing next to him and said, "Get her out of there now!"

Everyone worked to get her free and on the gurney. Once she was strapped down, he brushed the hair from her forehead and bent down to whisper in her ear. "I love you, Jamie. Please baby, don't leave me. I can't live without you."

Hot tears scalded his cheeks when he softly kissed her lips. He swore her fingers grasped his for a moment before the paramedics pushed her into the ambulance and they slammed the door behind them.

Chapter Thirteen

"Daddy?"

Wyatt spun around as he heard Samantha behind him. Chase had dropped him off at the hospital and he stood pacing the waiting room like an expectant father. He opened his arms as he said, "Come here, pumpkin."

She rubbed her tear stained face against his chest when he wrapped his arms around her and held her tight. "Is she going to be okay?"

"I don't know, Sam."

Samantha looked up at him with her trusting eyes. "But you are a doctor. How come you don't know?"

"I'm not working right now. They won't let me back there so I don't know what's going on."

"Why won't they let you back there?"

"I'm nothing to her, Sammy. I'm not her husband, father, brother... nothing."

"But you love her!"

He closed his eyes for a moment, but when he reopened them, Samantha stared at him with eyes so much like his own. "Yeah, baby, I do, but that's not enough for them."

The panel separating him from Jamie opened and Stacy poked her head out and said, "Doctor Crossland? You want to come back?"

"Yeah." He looked at Sam and then back to the nurse. "Is it okay for her daughter to come back there, too?" He hoped his face conveyed to Stacy that if things looked bad, he didn't want Samantha back there.

"She's okay doc. Come on." As they walked, Stacy said, "There is a chest tube so you might want to prepare Samantha for that."

"What does she mean, Dad?"

Before he answered he asked the nurse, "Did she have a collapsed lung?"

"Yeah. Good call on your part."

His gaze found Samantha again when they stopped outside the trauma bay. "Sam. Your mom's lung wasn't expanding like it should so they had to put a tube in her chest to help it. I know it's going to look scary, but I'll be right here with you, okay?"

Samantha nodded and he took her hand in his before he pulled the curtain aside.

Jamie was still strapped to the backboard when they approached. Her eyes were closed, but her chest rose and fell with even breaths. They walked to her side and Samantha took Jamie's hand in hers. Her voice cracked when she whispered, "Mommy?" He hadn't realized until right then how young their daughter really was.

"I don't know if she is awake yet, pumpkin."

"Wyatt?"

Jamie's voice came out in a murmur when her eyes opened slightly and he kissed her forehead. He bent over and whispered in her ear, "I'm right here, baby."

She licked her lips. "Where am I?"

"You're in the emergency room."

"What happened?"

"You were in a car accident."

"Samantha?"

"She's right here with me."

"She wasn't in the car?"

"No." He frowned, somewhat confused by her words. "You don't remember?"

"No."

"I'm sure you have a concussion so it's not surprising you don't remember, but Sam's right here."

"Mommy?"

Jamie's gaze found their daughter. "Hey, baby."

"Are you going to be okay, Mom?"

"I'll be fine. Right, Wyatt?"

"I don't think they have all the tests back yet, but it's a good sign that you are awake and talking."

Frown lines settled between Jamie's eyebrows as she asked, "What aren't you tell me?"

"Nothing...I..."

Doctor Hamilton popped his head through the curtains and gave Wyatt a worried look. "Hey, Wyatt. I want to show you something. Can you come out to the desk?"

"Sure." He kissed Jamie on the lips and told both her and Samantha he would be right back before he disappeared through the opening and approached the desk. "What is it?"

"Take a look at this CAT scan for me."

Wyatt took the chair and rolled the mouse through the images. He stopped on one picture for a moment, before he rolled back and forth between the first image and the third image so he could compare the three.

"There is some kind of growth showing up on the middle image," Doctor Hamilton said over his shoulder. "I can't tell exactly what it is."

"A tumor?"

"I can't tell, but this patient needs to be immediately referred to a neurologist. Wouldn't you agree?"

"Of course. They will probably need to do a biopsy and see what's going on. Is this patient having symptoms?"

"Yes and no."

"Huh?"

"Not always. Some syncope, dizziness, headaches..."

Wyatt's heart slammed against his ribs as it raced out of control. *Jamie.* He hadn't paid attention to the name on the scan until then. His gaze found the name at the top of screen and tears gathered in his eyes. He looked at his friend and colleague as the other doctor put a comforting hand on his shoulder. "You haven't said anything to her."

"No. I thought maybe you might want to. If not, I can, but she needs a specialist. She probably had one of her spells while she was driving and that's what caused the accident."

"I knew it! She's been so damned stubborn about going to the doctor to get checked out." He slammed his fist against the desk and several pairs of eyes stopped on him. "She has an appointment in a couple of days." He raked his hands over his face.

"You know you can't jump to conclusions, Wyatt. No one knows what's going on until they do some more tests."

"Are her neck and back clear?"

"Yeah. She can come off the backboard."

Wyatt looked over his shoulder when he heard voices coming up the hall. Charles, Bonnie, Chase and Abby moved toward the curtained off area where Jamie lay.

Great! Now I have to break this to her whole family!

"Do you want me to tell them?"

"No. It's okay. I'll do it. Hopefully it will go easier with me telling them." He stood and took a step in the direction of the trauma bay.

"Hang tough, man. This won't be easy."

"Thanks, Dale."

Wyatt moved with a heavy heart toward where Jamie lay.

How am I going to tell her this?

He stopped for a moment, trying to collect his nerve before he pushed the curtain aside and moved to her side.

"Can I get off this damned board now?"

He laughed softly. "Yeah. Let me help you." Wyatt removed the straps holding her down.

"Oh my gosh, that feels heavenly," she said, slipping her hand behind her neck. "Did they say what happened?"

"Doctor Hamilton thinks you might have had one of your passing out spells and lost control of the truck."

She dropped her gaze for a moment before it returned to his face. "I…I don't remember."

"I'm sure you are fine, Jamie," Bonnie said sternly, but when Wyatt's gaze met Abby's, he could see the worried frown on her face as she grasped her husband's hand.

Abby knows something isn't right.

"Bonnie, Charles—you two might want to sit down. I need to tell you all something and it's not going to be easy." He held out his hand to Samantha and pulled her to his side so she stood between him and Jamie.

"Wyatt. You're scaring me," Jamie whispered.

"Baby, listen. I know you've been having these episodes where you lose consciousness. You did it outside that night when Sam found out I am her father. These headaches you've been having on top of all that—well, baby, there isn't any easy way to say this." He squeezed her hand and held on tight. "Jamie, honey, there is something showing up on the CAT scan."

"What do you mean there is something on the scan?"

"I can't tell what it is and neither can Dale—I mean Doctor Hamilton. I know you have an appointment in a couple of days with Doctor Melton, the neurologist, but you need to see him tomorrow."

"Wyatt?" Tears rolled down her cheeks. "What are you saying?"

"Jamie, listen to me. I don't know what's wrong."

"But you're a doctor!" she exclaimed, before she pulled her hand from his. "Or is it you just don't want to tell me!"

Pushing the hair back from her cheek, he stroked it with his fingers. "God, Jamie, don't do this. I would tell you if I could, but I can't because I don't know. This isn't my specialty. All I can say is there is something showing up on your scan—something that's not normally there."

"A tumor?" Chase asked, his voice cracking.

His heart clenched in his chest. "I can't say, Chase."

"I want to go home," Jamie said as she pulled away from him. "Now!"

"You have to stay here tonight and let them keep an eye on you. The chest tube. You had a collapsed lung. You have to stay here."

"Then get this damned thing out of me!"

"Jamie—don't."

A gut-wrenching sob shook her frame and he gathered her in his arms. "Ssshhh. Everything will be okay. We'll get through this together."

She fisted his shirt in her hands and he could feel her tears on his chest. His throat threatened to close while he fought his own tears.

It's just not fair! I've just found her again and now this!

Wyatt's eyes met the watery gaze of Stacy over Jamie's head.

"We have a room for her upstairs. We should be moving her shortly."

He nodded and tried to pull back, but Jamie wasn't going to let him go.

Dale came in behind them and he mouthed over her head to give her something to calm her. The other man nodded and disappeared. Wyatt ran his hands down her back and whispered in her ear. He didn't say anything in particular, but he wanted her to know he would be there, no matter what.

Stacy came in a moment later with the injection in her hand and slowly pushed the medication through the IV tube in Jamie's arm.

A minute later, Jamie lifted her head and stared into his eyes. "You told them to give me something, didn't you?"

He brushed the hair back off her shoulder. "Yeah."

"That wasn't very nice, you know."

"You needed something."

"Now I'll just sleep, though, and I don't want to sleep." Her features relaxed as the medication took hold. "Don't leave me," she whispered, grasping his hand like it was her lifeline.

He leaned down and kissed her forehead. "Never."

Once she started to snore softly, he motioned for the rest of her family to follow him out into the hall. He raked his finger through his hair before he pulled Samantha to his side and wrapped his arm around her.

"What do we do now, Wyatt?" Charles asked, grasping Bonnie's hand in his.

"We wait."

Chase's voice rose in agitation and he almost shouted, "Wait? You have to be kidding me?"

"Chase, keep your voice down, please. Honey, Wyatt is doing what's best for Jamie. We have to believe that." Abby tried to reassure her husband with her words, but Wyatt could tell by the tightness around her mouth she was just as worried as the rest of them.

"There isn't anything more that can be done tonight, Chase. The neurologist will see her in the morning, look over her scan and go from there."

"This isn't fucking right! You're a doctor and she's a nurse that works here!"

"I can't pull strings with another doctor. He will have to see the scan. Her condition is stable. I plan to stay with her tonight here at the hospital and I will call if there are any changes. I don't expect any problems during the night. This isn't something that just showed up overnight. It's been going on for a while, from what I've heard."

"I can't believe this," Chase whispered, and Abby stepped in front of him, wrapping her arms around his waist.

Wyatt put his hand on Chase's shoulder. "I love her, too. I'll do everything in my power to protect her. You have to know that."

"I know, Wyatt. This just isn't fair."

"No, it's not, but we'll deal with it. Together."

Stacy moved up behind them and touched Wyatt on the arm. "We're going to move her upstairs now. Are you coming?"

"Yes. I'll be right behind you."

* * * *

Wyatt sat in the chair near the window while he watched Jamie sleep. His mind raced with the possibilities and terror gripped his heart when he thought about the worst-case scenario. A brain tumor. A cancerous brain tumor.

Silent tears slid down his cheeks. *Please God, don't take her away from me. I'll do anything. If you must take someone, take me. Sammy needs her mother.*

She moaned before her eyes opened and she whispered, "Wyatt?"

He quickly moved to the bed and sat beside her. "I'm right here, baby."

"What time is it?"

"Somewhere around two, I think," he whispered.

She scooted over to one side of the bed. "Lay here with me."

"The nurses will have a fit, you know."

"Like I give a shit. I want you to hold me."

He chuckled softly before he lay down beside her and wrapped his arm around her shoulder, pulling her against his side. When her head rested on his chest, he sighed in contentment.

After several minutes, her fingers pulled at the bottom of the t-shirt he wore. "What are you doing?"

"I want to feel your skin. Get this shirt off."

He growled. "That's not a good idea."

"Why not?"

"We're in the hospital and if you start touching me, I won't be able to keep my hands off you."

She lifted her head and shot a glance at the door. "Is there a lock on there?"

Air whooshed from his lungs as blood shunted to his groin. "No."

"Damn," she grumbled, but continued to pull his shirt up until she had it bunched up under his armpits. A contented sigh left her lips as she laid her head on his bare chest. "Much better."

"You're killing me here."

"Mmm…well you are the one who put a stop to anything else, mister."

"I really don't want to be the center of the gossip between the nurses come morning."

She lifted her head and looked him in the eye. "Gossip? We don't gossip."

A snort of disbelief left his lips.

Jamie punched him in the rib.

"Hey!"

"You deserved that," she said before she lay back down. "Where's Sam?"

"With your mom and dad."

"Is she upset?"

"Of course she's upset. She doesn't understand what's going on. All she knows is her mom is in the hospital and they don't know what the problem is."

"And that her dad can't fix it?"

"Yeah."

Silence enveloped them in a warm cocoon of intimacy as she stroked the hair on his chest with her fingers.

"I'm scared," she whispered against his skin.

"I know, baby." His palm traced her shoulder and down her arm. "I need to say something, Jamie, but I don't want you to think it's because of what's going on."

She sat up and frowned. "Okay."

"I love you. I never stopped loving you in the last nine years. It tore my heart apart to leave before, but I'm warning you right now, Jamie Marie Wilder, I'm in this until death do us part. If you can't say you love me…" She pressed her finger to his lips to stop his words as a silent tear rolled down her cheek.

"I love you, Wyatt. I know I told you back then I didn't, but I did. You've had my heart in the palm of your hand since I was seventeen. I can't take back what happened before. I wish I had never sent you away, but that's water under the bridge. All I want now is to spend the rest of my life with you and raise our daughter together." A watery chuckle spilled from her lips. "And maybe make a few more babies with you—God willing."

He kissed her fingertips and then pulled her hand away from his mouth. "He has to, Jamie. I can't lose you—not when we just found our way back to each other. I don't think He's that cruel."

"I hope not, Wyatt," she whispered as she put her head back on his chest.

* * * *

Pink and purple streaked across the sky outside the window of Jamie's hospital room as the sun struggled to make its way over the hills in the distance. The steady thump of Wyatt's heart in her ear calmed her like nothing else could. His soft snores echoed in the room. He needed to rest. He hadn't slept all night until about an hour ago when he finally had given into exhaustion.

Letting her fingers drift through the silky hair on his chest, she wondered if today she would have the answers she sought.

*Please God. I know I haven't been the perfect daughter or the perfect mother to Samantha and I know what I did to Wyatt wasn't fair, but…*she fought against the tears that threatened to fall. *I don't want to lose him now and I'm terrified he won't be able to handle this. I love him so much.*

"Baby, don't cry," he murmured against the top of her head.

Tears choked the words in her throat. She squeezed his waist momentarily and then her hand returned to the muscles beneath her cheek.

The hospital room door squeaked open as Doctor Melton poked his head inside. He cocked a questioning eyebrow in their direction and Wyatt sat up and moved to the chair. "Anyone awake in here?"

"Yeah, Mark. Come on in."

"How is our patient today?"

"Scared out of my mind," she answered, and Wyatt squeezed her hand.

Doctor Melton took the chair on the other side of the bed, and opened her chart. "Well, let's see what we can figure out. I've looked at your CAT scan and truthfully, I don't like what I see."

She gasped as terror rolled down her back in a shiver. Wyatt grasped her hand between both of his.

"You need to know, Jamie, I won't be able to tell anything without doing surgery."

"Surgery? What do you mean surgery?"

"I need to do a biopsy on the tumor in your head."

"It is a tumor?" Wyatt asked.

"Appears to be. Now whether it's cancerous or not—I can't tell without a biopsy."

"Is that what's been causing her headaches and dizzy spells?"

"Yes. It's pressing on her spinal cord, so more than likely we'll have to remove it whether it's cancerous or not." He turned his attention back to her. "We can do it all at once if that is what you want, Jamie."

Oh God! Surgery? Cut my head open? She started to shake, her hand trembling inside Wyatt's and he moved back to sit beside her on the bed.

"Are there any other options, Mark?"

"Afraid not."

"When?"

"Soon. Like in a day or two."

"Wyatt?" Her voice cracked with unshed tears.

"It's okay, baby. Everything will be fine." His focus returned to the other man as trepidation ran down her back. "We have to discuss this with her family before any decisions are made."

"Of course." Doctor Melton stood. "Page me when you've decided."

Wyatt stroked her arm for a few minutes while they let the silence envelope them. "We need to call your family."

She nodded and he reached beside him to pick up his cell phone.

What will Samantha say?

The sound of his voice telling her family they needed to come to the hospital faded from her ears as she thought about their daughter.

How is Sam going to deal with this?

Wyatt set his phone back on the nightstand and wrapped his arms around her. "They'll be here in about an hour."

Neither of them moved as they waited.

Chase burst into the room, with Abby on his heels and Jeremiah on her hip. Charles and Bonnie weren't far behind.

"Where is Samantha?" Jamie asked.

"She's at Ashley's. I didn't think we should bring her here for this."

"So…what did the doctor say?" Bonnie asked.

Jamie took a deep breath. "It will require surgery."

"What! Surgery?" Chase yelled.

"Chase, please. Keep your voice down. There are other patients up here," Jamie reprimanded and her brother slumped in the chair.

"We need to get the rest of the family on the phone and talk about this," Chase said, grabbing his phone and dialing Justin, Katrina, Cole and Carrie before he put them all on conference call on his phone.

"What do mean a tumor? What the hell is going on there?" Justin's voice growled into the phone.

"Let Wyatt explain. He knows better than anyone," Jamie said, then scrunched her face as her other two brothers yelled simultaneously into the phone.

"What the hell is he doing there?"

"I'll explain later, but just know this. He's here to stay, so forget trying to kill him. That goes for all three of you," she said as she pinned Chase to the chair.

"You didn't bother to tell us this little piece of information, Chase? How long have you known?" Justin asked.

"Long enough," Chase answered.

"Listen," Wyatt began, "we can stand here all day and argue about my relationship with Jamie or we can discuss the problem at hand. Jamie has a tumor in her brain that is pressing on her spinal cord. She has to have surgery to remove it. We won't know until they take it out and do a biopsy on the tissue whether there is more to worry about."

Jamie cleared her throat. "This is my decision. The surgery will happen as quickly as Doctor Melton can schedule it."

"But Jamie…" Cole started to argue.

"No, Cole. I have to do this. He basically told me there was no other option."

"I don't believe this," Cole murmured. "Carrie and I will be there tomorrow, then."

"You don't have to come," Jamie replied, but deep inside she wanted her family with her.

"Yes, we do, Jamie. We'll leave this afternoon and be there by tomorrow morning. I need to go. I've got to make arrangements for the store. I love to, sis. Hang tough, okay?"

"I love you too, Cole. See you tomorrow."

She heard one click.

"Jamie? Katrina and I will catch the first plane we can."

"Okay," Jamie whispered tearfully. "Make sure you bring that nephew of mine. I haven't seen him yet."

Justin chuckled. "Of course. Like Kat would come without him."

Jamie laughed. "I know. I love you, big brother."

"I love you too, Jamie. See you in a little while."

"Bye, Justin."

Chapter Fourteen

The hospital room was filled to the brink with bodies. Justin, Katrina and their small son, Max, sat in the left corner. Cole was in the other corner, with Carrie next to him and Anne on her mother's lap while Cole held onto a squirming Robert. Charles and Bonnie had taken two chairs next to Jamie's bed. Chase and Abby stood against the wall, with Jeremiah in Abby's arms.

Wyatt sat next to Jamie on the bed with Samantha standing next to him. He didn't like the looks he was receiving from Jamie's brothers as they shot daggers at him from their respective corners. He had an agenda today and they were just going to have to accept it.

"So, what's the plan here?" Justin asked.

Jamie looked at him before she turned her attention back to her brother. "Surgery will be day after tomorrow. They'll remove the tumor, biopsy it and hopefully, it will be benign."

"Speak English here for us non-medical personnel, Jamie," Cole said.

"Non-cancerous, Cole."

"We've already made room for everyone at the Rocking W," Chase told the group. "I'm assuming all of you are staying until after the surgery."

"Of course," the group said in chorus.

"How long will it take to get the results of the biopsy?" Carrie asked.

Jamie looked up at Wyatt and he replied, "It could take several weeks, but I know Dr. Melton pretty well. I've already asked him to push the pathologist for an emergency result. Hopefully, we'll have some good news the day of the surgery."

"They can tell that fast?"

Wyatt wasn't sure who the question came from, but he answered, "Yes. In some cases."

Silence prevailed in the room as each person absorbed the ramifications.

"There is something I need to say to all of you, so please hear me out. I know you all were very angry at how things went down between Jamie and me when she got pregnant with Samantha. Chase knows what actually happened and I'm sure he's shared it with you, Justin and Cole. You all must know that even with how things happened, I don't fault Jamie for it and I take responsibility, to some extent, for the mess as well."

"You should," Justin growled.

"That's enough out of you, husband of mine," Katrina told him.

Wyatt ignored Justin's words and stood. Samantha moved slightly to his left as she watched with tears in her eyes and he winked at her. Their daughter had been instrumental in helping him with the arrangements.

He went down on one knee and took Jamie's hand in his as he reached inside his shirt pocket. "I know this isn't probably the best time and it certainly isn't moonlight and roses, but it's something I should have done a long time ago. You know I love you with all my heart and I know you love me too. We had that conversation the other night."

A watery chuckle escaped from between her lips as she shook her head and whispered, "Yes, we did."

He held the diamond ring in front of her that he and Samantha had picked out the day before and asked, "Jamie Marie Wilder, will you marry me?"

Tears rolled down her cheeks as a huge smile rippled across her lips. "I love you, Wyatt."

"Is that a yes?"

"Say yes, Mom."

Jamie laughed at Samantha's words before she leaned over, kissed him on the lips. When she finally lifted her mouth from his, she said, "Yes."

He slipped the ring on her left hand and she kissed him again. Lost in the feel of her lips on his, it took a moment for it to register in his brain that her family still stood nearby.

"There's one more thing, Mom."

"What's that baby?"

"Tell her, Dad."

He smiled at Samantha before his attention returned to Jamie. "I've made arrangements for us to get married in the chapel downstairs if you want. I want you for my wife before the surgery, if you'll have me. If you want a big wedding, we can have one after you are better."

"I want to marry you right now, right this minute, but will tomorrow work?"

A smile spread across his face. "It's perfect."

Jamie's eyes moved to Abby and she held out her hand. "Abby? Will you stand up with me?"

"Me?"

The surprise on Abby's face made him laugh as Jamie said, "Yes, you."

"I'd be happy to, Jamie."

Wyatt looked at Chase. "I know you don't like me much, Chase, but I don't have a lot of friends here in town yet. Will you be my best man?"

"As long as Jamie is happy, I wouldn't stand in your way. Yeah. I'd be honored to be your best man."

Wyatt's attention moved back to Jamie. "Baby, I know you'd like to pick out flowers and all that, but Samantha has already taken care of it and even picked out a dress for you."

"She did, did she?" Samantha's head bobbed up and down in affirmation. "Well then, I'm sure it will be perfect."

* * * *

The wedding went off without a hitch and even some of the staff members of the hospital attended. They had a small reception in the hospital doctor's lounge and invited anyone and everyone to the party. Jamie was stunning in an off-the-shoulder white gown as she carried a bouquet of white and pink roses. Wyatt stood proudly at the altar in a black tux. They said their vows in front of her family and his. He had called his parents and siblings after he had asked Jamie to marry him and most of them actually made it to the wedding.

Wyatt held her in his arms as they swayed to the music playing softly in the background. "I love you," he whispered softly against her ear.

"I love you, too."

"You have no idea how much I want to make love to you right now."

"Oh, yes, I do. I want that more than anything. I wonder if the staff would say anything if we blocked the door to my hospital room."

He threw back his head and laughed. "You don't have to wonder."

"Huh?"

"I've convinced Doctor Melton to let you out, just for tonight, so we can have a proper honeymoon, or at least a wedding night, anyway."

"Are you kidding? Really?"

"Uh-huh. We have reservations in a pretty swanky hotel downtown. Honeymoon suite and all."

Tears welled up in her eyes and rolled softly down her cheeks. He brushed them away with his thumb. "Why the tears?"

"Because I love you so much and I'm so scared this will be our last time together."

"Don't say that, baby. Everything will be fine."

"But what if it's not, Wyatt? What if I don't make it through the surgery? What if…" He put his finger on her lips to stop her words.

"No more 'what ifs'. We'll deal with whatever happens—later. Tonight is our wedding night and as such, I plan to enjoy your body immensely until the wee hours of the morning." He stepped back and took her hand in his as he addressed the crowd around them. "Folks, Jamie and I are going to leave. Enjoy yourselves for as long as you like. The hospital has given us free-reign on the room." He let his gaze sweep her family. "We will see all of you in the morning, I'm sure."

"We'll be right here," Bonnie said as she leaned over and kissed Jamie. "Be happy, sweetheart. You deserve it."

"I love you, Mom and Dad." She kissed her parents and returned to take Wyatt's hand in hers. "I'll see you tomorrow."

* * * *

Jamie slowly opened her eyes when she felt fingers stroking her face.

"Come on, baby. Open those beautiful brown eyes for me."

She groaned softly and tried to open one eye, but the glare of the light over her head made her eyes hurt. The tickle of fingers in the hair near her ear annoyed her and she tried to turn her head from the sensation.

"Come on, Mrs. Crossland. I need you to open your eyes."

"Leave me alone, Wyatt. I'm trying to sleep."

He chuckled and said, "Nope. Not until you look at me."

"Fine," she grumbled and opened one eye to see him sitting next to her. "Better?"

"You can do better than that. I want to see both of them."

"Damn, you're a pest." She opened both eyes just far enough she could see him. "Happy now?"

"Much better. How do you feel?"

"Like I've been hit by a Mack truck."

"Are you hurting anywhere?"

"Not really, just sleepy. Is the surgery over?"

"Yeah. You did fabulous."

"Where's Sam?"

"Right here, Mom."

Jamie turned her head so she could see her daughter. "Hi, baby."

"Are you okay?"

"I'll be fine, Sammy." She turned and looked at Wyatt again. "Did they get it all?" Moisture gathered in the corners of his eyes and terror gripped her heart. "Wyatt?"

He grasped her fingers so tight she thought for sure he would break them. "Yeah, baby, they did. And you know what else?"

"What?"

"It's benign. You're going to be fine."

"Thank the Lord above."

"You got that right, sis."

For the first time, she noticed her brothers and their wives hovering nearby. "You guys just couldn't wait, huh?" Jamie chuckled.

"Nope. We had to find out just as soon as Wyatt knew. I guess since you two are married now, we'll have to put up with him for a long time to come," Justin replied.

Her gaze found the wonderful face of her husband as she caressed the side of his face. "You bet."

Epilogue

"Come on, baby. You need to push with the next one," Wyatt said behind her as he braced her back.

Jamie groaned softly. "Why in the hell did I ever let you convince me to have another baby?"

His laughter ruffled the hair at her ear. "Because you love me."

"You got me there, Doctor Crossland." She moaned as the next contraction rolled across her abdomen and Wyatt ran his hands over her stomach. "God, I forgot how much this hurts!"

"You're doing great."

"If you would like to trade places with me, just say the word."

"I would if I could, Jamie, you know that, but if it helps, I love you."

"It doesn't help, Wyatt, but I love you anyway."

"Okay, Jamie. One more good push and the head will be through," Doctor Archer said from between Jamie's legs.

When the next contraction hit her, she pulled her knees up to her chest and pushed with everything she had. "Oh, God!" she screamed as the baby's head slipped through.

"Don't push now. Let me get the shoulders."

"Breathe, baby," he whispered in her ear. "Short, easy breaths. It's almost over."

"All right. One last push with the next one and we'll have ourselves a baby. Ready?"

Jamie took one large, deep breath, pulling as much air into her lungs as she possibly could and with the next contraction, she bared down. Relief washed over her as she felt the baby slip free from her body and a healthy scream echo through the room.

"You've got a girl."

"A girl?" she whispered in a ragged breath.

A warm tear wet her cheek as Wyatt murmured behind her. "A beautiful baby girl."

"I guess that's all you know how to make, eh, Daddy?" Jamie teased as the doctor started to clean her up and the nurse took care of their daughter.

"We'll just have to try again, then, won't we?"

"Ask me that in about three years. Let's get this one out of diapers before we think of any more."

"As long as we can practice numerous times between now and then, I'm all for waiting."

"You are incorrigible, you know that?"

"Mmm...I happen to love my wife and find her irresistibly sexy." He kissed her. "Is that a crime these days?"

"Nope." Her face sobered.

"What's wrong?"

"I just hope you aren't disappointed we didn't have a boy."

"Why would you think that? I love our daughters—both of them, because they are a part of the two of us. We'll worry about a boy later on and even if we never have one, that's okay too." His eyes held the truth of his words as his love shone bright for her to see.

"I love you, Wyatt."

"I love you too, Jamie Crossland. Don't you ever think I don't. It doesn't matter whether our children are boys or girls and I'm sure both of these two will keep us on our toes for years to come."

"I'm so glad you came back to Laramie."

"Me too, baby, me too."

THE END

www.romancestorytime.com

ABOUT THE AUTHOR

Sandy Sullivan is a romance author, who, when not writing, spends her time with her husband Shaun on their farm in middle Tennessee. She loves to ride her horses, play with their dogs and relax on the porch, enjoying the rolling hills of her home south of Nashville. Country music is a passion of hers and she loves to listen to it while she writes.

She's an avid reader of romance novels and enjoys reading, Nora Roberts, Jude Deveraux, Susan Wiggs, Tonya Ramagos and many others. Finding new authors and delving into something different helps feed the need for literature. A registered nurse by education, she loves to help people and spread the enjoyment of romance to those around her with her novels. She loves cowboys so you'll find many of her novels have sexy men in tight jeans and cowboy boots.

Also by Sandy Sullivan

Cowboy Love
Wilder Series 1: *Wild Wyoming Nights*
Wilder Series 2: *Wild Rodeo Nights*
Wilder Series 3: *Wild Nevada Ride*
BookStrand Mainstream: *Love's Sweet Surrender*
BookStrand Mainstream: *Texas Lady*

Available at
BOOKSTRAND.COM

Siren Publishing, Inc.
www.SirenPublishing.com

Breinigsville, PA USA
21 November 2010
249792BV00003B/23/P